DREAMING OF HOME

THE LONG ROAD HOME
BOOK TWENTY

CAITLYN O'LEARY

The Binge Read Babes
Cat Johnson, Abbie Zanders, Maryann Jordan, and Kris Michaels
You Ladies Have Saved My Sanity, My Heart, and My Life

SYNOPSIS

**Finding the twin I never knew I had? -- Easy.
Protecting the love of my life? That's going to take
everything I've got.**

Kai Davies
You're supposed to be able to trust your father, right?
Nope. I always knew he was an evil so-and-so, but
lying to me about who I was? That was a new low. So
here I am in Jasper Creek, Tennessee trying to find
out if the dreams that have plagued me all my life are
real. Do I really have a twin brother? What is he like?
And what can I tell him after all the years of
deception?

Marlowe Jones
Teaching is all I ever wanted to do. When school
bullies viciously attacked a girl, it was second-nature
for me to step in and stop it. Little did I know how

far the bullies' powerful parents would go to destroy my life. Getting fired from my private school was only the beginning. Now I'm here in Jasper Creek, Tennessee, five hundred miles away from home, keeping my head down and trying to settle into a quiet little life. Easy, if it weren't for the gorgeous and fascinating Kai Davies, with secrets of his own.

Just when I figure out how to fit Kai into my life, my past finds me, rearing its ugly head, and I mean ugly. Kai is determined to be my hero, but I don't need one. I'll handle everything myself like I always do. Then ugly turns to frightening, and frightening turns to deadly and then I turn to Kai. But is it too late?

PROLOGUE

One step at a time. Just one step at a time.

How often had I been saying that to myself? Months?

Fuck, I'd been saying something close to that since I was ten years old and Dad told me to sink or swim. Literally.

I pulled my half-filled duffel off the baggage carousel and grimaced. How absolutely shitty was this? I knew down to the pound how much it weighed. Scratch that. I knew down to the ounce. Fourteen pounds and ten ounces. My backpack weighed ten pounds and six ounces. Mike, my physical therapist, had weighed them both since I was only cleared to lift twenty-five pounds. I knew he was just making a point, but he was really close to getting a throat punch. Except for the fact he was bigger, faster and in much better shape, and I'd be on my ass in less than a second.

Then the bastard had the nerve to tell me not to buy a book or anything when I was at the airport, or I'd go over my weight limit.

What an asshole.

I hated this shit.

Meanwhile, Clay Alvers down at Fort Liberty in North Carolina was also being a major pain in my ass. We were recruited for Delta Force at the same time and eventually roomed together. He took care of everything when they didn't know if I was going to live or die.

When they eventually figured out I was going to live and sent my ass to Walter Reed to be operated on, he managed all my finances and basically held my life together. But when I realized I'd never be able to go back to the teams, I told him to either give my shit away or throw it away, since I wasn't going back to North Carolina.

But no.

Instead, the asshole ships me a key to a storage unit and a copy of a check that he'd made out to himself from my account. He'd put in the memo line of the check, *management of large and disgruntled mammals.*

That was one of the first things that'd made me smile since I'd realized just how fucked-up my back was. On the last mission I was on in a war-torn city in Eastern Europe, multiple bullet fragments had punctured my upper spine. The doctors kept telling me that with physical therapy and working with a doctor who specialized in pain management, I could lead a normal life. There would be discomfort and I wouldn't have the same mobility as I used to, but it would be a normal life.

Great, that meant I could become a drugged-out insurance salesman.

Oh joy.

I accessed my airline app on my phone, hoping that I had gotten the earlier flight to Nashville, so I didn't have a six-hour layover here in Atlanta, but no such luck.

I was stuck.

I went out onto the concourse to see if I could find one of those neck pillows that the guy in the seat beside me had been using on my last flight. He snored all the way from Dulles, so maybe it worked. It didn't look like it weighed too much, so Mike wouldn't have an aneurism if I bought one.

When I left the shop, I had four magazines, a bottle of water, a Butterfinger candy bar and one of those neck pillows. They only had pink, but at this point, I didn't care. All that mattered was that maybe I wouldn't have to take another one of those fucking pain pills.

I looked around to see if there was a restaurant or someplace I could sit down and grab a bite to eat when I got a text.

Demon from Hell: *You better not have bought a book.*

I looked down at my four magazines. *Forbes, Bon*

Appétit, *Popular Science* and *The Economist* weighed far more than a paperback.

Me: *Nope, no book.*

Demon from Hell: *No beer.*

Me: *So, you think I've lost brain cells now, huh? You think I'm going to mix alcohol and narcotics. Thanks for the vote of confidence, Mike.*

Demon from Hell: *Toughen up. I'm texting cause I want you to meet a friend of mine.*

I rolled my eyes.

Me: *I don't need one more person checking up on me.*

Demon from Hell: *The world doesn't revolve around you, Kai. I'm serious. Head for the USO and check in on Blessing. She's one of the best people you're ever going to meet. Just make sure she's doing okay.*

Me: *Blessing? What kind of name is that?*

Demon from Hell: *What kind of name is Kai? Go in gentle, will you? Give her a hug. Tell her it's from me.*

I squeezed the bridge of my nose.

Me: *All right, but you owe me.*

Demon from Hell: *It's the other way around, and once you pull your head out of your ass, you'll know it.*

Me: *Gotta go.*

I shoved my phone into my rucksack and headed upstairs to the mezzanine. The sad part was I had pulled my head out of my ass and I did know how much I owed Mike. After my last surgery, there was some kind of nerve connectivity issue with my right foot. The docs couldn't figure out what had happened, so they couldn't go cutting on me to fix it. They said PT was my only option.

In came Mike Kowalski. Former linebacker for the Philadelphia Eagles. He'd gotten hit one too many times in the knee. Went back to college and graduated as a Doctor of Physical Therapy. Ended up at Walter Reed hospital, and I ended up with him. He was a demon from hell. He was also a godsend. I ended up walking within three months. Riding a bike in five. But my back and neck were still issues. It was going to take a while before the docs would lift the medical restrictions. Hence, there I was, lifting twenty-five pounds of shit and some magazines and water, and my fluffy pink pillow.

I saw the sign for the USO and followed it until I got to the doors. Inside stood a woman anywhere between thirty-five to fifty-five staring at me with a wide smile.

"Well, come on in," she said with a subtle Southern accent that soothed me immediately.

"Your name wouldn't be Blessing, would it?" I asked.

She smiled brighter. God knew how that was possible. "Well, yes, it is." Her forehead crinkled as she looked at me. "Have we met before?"

"Nope. I was just told by a mutual friend to ask for a woman named Blessing."

"Isn't that wonderful. Who's our friend?"

"Mike Kowalski. Big guy, used to—"

"Oh, you don't have to tell me about him," she laughed. "I've missed that man. Rarely do you run into a soul like his, and when you do, you treasure them."

She got a faraway look on her face. Then she shook her head as if to clear it and bit her lip. "Is he still working at Walter Reed?"

I gave a stiff little nod. It was the best I could do.

"And you, did he take good care of you?"

"In that gentle way of his," I sighed.

Blessing threw back her head and laughed. "Oh my. I'll just bet." She took a quick moment to look me up and down. "Gentle," she chuckled again. "Just like your military training I assume," she murmured.

She had me there. The special forces training was no joke. But there was something about wondering if one of your appendages would be paralyzed for the rest of your life that ate at you and was a worse mind fuck than the interrogation resistance training I'd gone through. At least until Mike had pulled me through to the other side.

"Sargeant?"

"Huh?"

Shit, I missed what she had been saying.

"Can I get you to sign into the book?"

Gingerly, I pulled my rucksack off my shoulder and dropped it to the floor, then I signed in. I pulled out my wallet to get her my ID and a well-worn picture fell out.

"I don't need your ID," Blessing said with a soft smile. She was looking at the picture.

6

"They're darling. May I?"

I shrugged.

She picked up the picture. "Carrot tops, but your hair just has a bit of auburn in it now. How old were the two of you when this was taken?"

I shrugged again.

She turned it over.

"Brady and Grady, Jasper Creek, Tennessee. Hmmm, sounds like a nice place." She handed me back my picture and I shoved the picture back into my wallet.

She looked down at my signature in the sign-in book and then back up at me. "You're Kai now, huh?"

I didn't know what to say, so I nodded.

"Kai, I know you think you've gone through the tough part, but you haven't. Trust your gut, Kai. You'll find some surprising allies if you're willing to let them in. They can make all the difference in the world."

Shit, did she have dreams, too? Or maybe this is just the beginning of dementia.

But I couldn't shut her out. Mike was worried about her. Was it because of this? Was he worried that she was losing her mind? *Damn.* She was so sweet and welcoming. No wonder he was worried.

"Well, let me take you back to a place I like to call the library. There are a couple of others who still have awhile to wait. Some of them are like you. They're injured and need some peace and quiet."

She got out from behind the desk and took my

arm. She definitely had that Southern charm I had always experienced in North Carolina. I just hated the fact that I had to give Mike bad news.

"Before we go, I have to do one last thing," I said.

"What's that?"

"Mike wanted me to give you a hug."

"Well, isn't that about the nicest thing that's happened all week?"

I bent down and wrapped my arms around her. She had a delicate perfume, not overwhelming. Yeah. A really gracious lady. Mike was right.

I looked around 'the library' and saw three men and a woman.

"The recliner is open," Blessing said. "That would probably be best for your back." I put my rucksack beside it, then frowned at Blessing.

"I never said I had a back injury."

"Didn't you? Well, how else would I have known about it?" She patted my arm. "Just let Kate know if you need anything. She's been here before and knows the lay of the land."

As soon as I sat down, the pretty woman offered me a piece of candy.

"Don't do it, man. That shit is a silent killer." A brown-haired man said to me.

I shook my head at the woman. She popped one

of the gummies in her mouth and squinted. They were obviously sour. I was glad I'd passed.

"So, where are you headed?" she asked.

"Tennessee. I have some things to do out there."

Yeah, like find out if I've lost my damned mind.

I lifted the leg rest of the recliner and sighed in relief as some of the pressure was let off my back and neck.

"Man, I feel that to my bones," a guy said in a New York accent. I watched as he tossed back either one or two pills from the bottle he was holding. "Anti-inflammatory pills only go so far," he said as he looked at me.

"Truth," I nodded stiffly.

I reached down to my rucksack and pulled out my pink neck pillow and placed it around my neck. I looked around the room. I saw each and every one of them struggling not to laugh.

"What? Pink's my favorite color."

I closed my eyes and started making a mental list of what I needed to do when I got to Nashville. My final destination was Jasper Creek. But first I needed to do some recon and prep work. I'd already procured some wheels, just needed to pick those up. American made, four-wheel-drive and manual transmission. What more could a man ask for?

I'd already checked birth records for twin boys in

Tennessee with the first names Brady and Grady. I was stunned to find four sets of twins born the year before, the year of, and the year after I was born with the names Brady and Grady. I'd checked the years before and after, just in case dear old dad had forged my birth year as well as my name on my birth certificate.

It didn't take much detective work. There were Grady and Brady Beaumont who were born in Gatlinburg, but their residence was Jasper Creek. A little more digging showed that Brady and Arthur Beaumont went missing when Brady was four years old. The missing persons case was still open.

I dug deeper and found that my mom, Rose Beaumont died when I was eighteen, and my brother Grady enlisted in the Marines.

So, I'd fly into Nashville, pick up my truck. Buy some clothes that would help me fit in a bit more, then look up some places online to stay in Jasper Creek, then get in my truck and drive.

I don't know when I drifted off to sleep, but I did.

It was one of the two dreams that plagued me almost every night.

I was sitting on the bottom step using a big branch to hit the dirt. I liked seeing the clouds of dirt float up.

"You're getting dirty. Mama wib be mad."

He was sitting up on the red porch swing so his church pants don't getted dirty. He always minded Mama. "So?" I grinned over my shoulder at Grady.

Grady laughed. So did I. Mama always laughed too. This wasn't a big bad. I never did big bads, just little bads. And anyway, our dad wasn't around, so we were safe.

"Brady. Grady. Time to go," Mama called from inside.

"I'm going," a different voice said. I woke up. I was in Atlanta. The USO.

Kate was saying goodbye to all of us. She stopped at the door of the library where all of us injured had been camping out. She looked at me.

"Just remember whatever Blessing told you today. Do it. Don't second-guess her. It will make your life so much easier."

She tapped on the door and stared directly at me. "Do it," she repeated. Then she was gone.

I pulled the tech magazine from my rucksack because I sure as hell didn't want to go back to sleep. The last thing I needed to do was have a nightmare in front of everybody here. I got lost in all the new gadgets featured in the Mobile World Congress. After all, who doesn't need a bendable Smartphone that you can wrap around your wrist?

I don't know how much time went by before my non-bendable phone buzzed. All the other guys had left but me, and now I saw that my plane finally had worked out a crew, so it would board soon. I gathered up my stuff.

"Oh, I see you got word."

I looked up to see Blessing smiling at me from the doorway to the library.

"I did. It looks like they'll start the boarding process in about forty-five minutes."

"Take some food to go. For those shorter flights, they have nothing but a bag of nuts or two little cookies."

"I just might do that."

I winced as I got up out of the chair. I really needed a pain pill, but for some reason I didn't want to take one in front of Blessing, which was horseshit. It shouldn't matter. Mike would kick my ass. He always said to stay in front of the pain. I pulled the prescription bottle out of my rucksack and shook my head when I saw Blessing holding out a bottle of water.

"Do you always know what's going to happen before it happens?"

"I just have a habit of reading situations. Most times I read them accurately." She shrugged as I took the bottle and popped the pill into my mouth.

"I hope you feel better by the time you board the plane," she said.

"That makes two of us." I paused. "Kate told us to do whatever you had to say, otherwise we would regret it."

Blessing threw back her head and laughed. "I like that woman."

"You told me that I should trust my gut and let

people in, and it would make all the difference in the world. What does that even mean?"

She held out her arm. "Walk with me."

I took her arm, and we walked down the hall to the front desk. A younger woman in a similar apron was talking to a Marine.

"Do you mind showing me that photo again?" Blessing asked.

I pulled out my wallet and gave her the tattered photo.

"Cute kids, Brady and Grady, huh?" She turned it over. "Jasper Creek. This is a good place. I feel it. I imagine that if a man is feeling aimless, he might find what he needs, even when he's not looking for it."

"That makes no sense. I *am* looking for something in Jasper Creek."

I was getting frustrated.

"But Kai, is it the right thing?" She looked down at her watch. "You better hurry. You don't want to miss your plane. Say hey to Mike for me."

I couldn't help it. I gave her another gentle hug. "I will. You take care."

Now I was even more worried about what I'd have to tell Mike.

1

I couldn't believe I'd left my phone in my classroom. What a dork. I'd been wanting to film this general assembly for weeks, and there I was, without my phone. I would have run, but I was wearing one of my cute pair of heels, and running wasn't an option, not on these linoleum floors.

Phone in hand, I was almost back to the assembly when I heard laughing. That was odd; everybody was supposed to be at the assembly, and this sounded like students.

"Kick her again."

That I heard clear as day. Then I heard a girl laughing. I kicked off my heels and started running, slipping, then running again, down the hall until I turned the corner. In an instant, I saw what was going on. Two girls had hold of another. One was dragging the girl down the hallway by her hair. The other girl was kicking at her. I saw a third girl who I recognized out of the corner of my eye. Cindy. She laughed as she filmed the attack.

"Stop this right now!" I roared.

The two girls assaulting the one girl froze. The girl holding the victim by her hair released her. The injured girl's head landed on the floor with a sickening thud. I ran to her as the two girls, one of whom I recognized, ran off.

When I got to the girl, she was moaning and trying to get up.

"Stay still, honey. Help is on the way. I looked around frantically. Cindy was standing a few feet away with her phone pointed towards us.

"Cindy, stop filming and call 911."

She giggled and continued to film.

"What's going on?"

I looked up and thanked God when I saw Sue Rankin rushing down the hall. She taught eleventh grade AP English and was one of my best friends. "Sue, call an ambulance. This girl has been hurt." I didn't bother to look to see if Sue was doing as I asked. I knew she would. Soon she was beside me.

"What happened?"

I pushed back the girl's hair and recognized her from my math class. Alice Daly. She was trying to get up again.

"Kim Laughton happened," I said bitterly. Everyone knew she was a bully. "She was dragging Alice down the hall by her hair. When I yelled, Kim dropped her. Alice hit her head hard, on the floor. I don't want to move her. The EMTs need to look her over."

Alice tried to move again. "I'm fine," she whispered. She looked different without her glasses. I looked around and spotted them at the end of the hall.

Sue gently encouraged Alice to stay lying down. That's when I heard more giggling. I looked up and saw Cindy was still filming.

I saw red.

I jumped up. "Give me that phone."

She stood there and laughed some more, holding it higher to film my face.

"Stop filming and give it to me *now*." I held out my hand.

"No way. This is my phone and I'm not giving it to anyone. Just wait 'til I put this up on the internet. I'll get so many likes."

I was past red, I was sick to my stomach, I lunged for the phone. "Give this to me, now."

She twisted away. "You don't have the right to take it from me. I'll tell my parents. You'll lose your job."

I yanked the phone out of her hand.

"Give that back to me," she shrieked. "That's my property."

I turned away and crouched down next to Alice. I stopped the video feed and sent the video to my cell phone, then I put it into my skirt pocket.

Cindy yanked at my arm, tearing my blouse. I shrugged her off me.

"Give me my phone!" she shrieked again. Alice whimpered and scuttled away from the sound of Cindy yelling. She was obviously terrified. I needed to get Cindy away from her.

I turned to Sue. "You got this?"

"Yeah," she muttered. "Take care of that mess." She pointed to Cindy.

I got up off the floor and turned my attention to Cindy. I advanced on her, and she backed up until her back hit the lockers.

"You wait until the principal hears about this. You, Kim, and the other girl will be expelled for the rest of the school year. You probably will be charged with assault."

Cindy paled. "I didn't do anything. Kim and Julie were the ones that hurt Alice, I just filmed. My parents won't let anything happen to me. You'll be fired for touching me."

"It's on camera. I didn't touch you."

"You can't prove anything. My dad won't let you do anything to me."

"I have the evidence, Cindy. I sent it to my phone."

"You can't do that!" She stamped her foot like she was in kindergarten.

"We're waiting for the authorities to arrive, we'll see what happens."

I could hear the sirens. I'd need to guide them to where we were. I didn't need to guard Cindy. I knew where to find her, plus I had the proof of what she did on her and my cell phones.

"You better stay here. It will be worse for you if the police have to hunt you down. I'm going to go get them so they can help Alice."

"They won't do anything to me," she taunted. "You're the one who's in trouble."

As soon as I started down the hall, I could hear her running. As I turned the corner I heard the student body returning to their classes. I hustled to rescue my shoes and make it to the EMTs.

By the time I got there, the principal and vice principal were already talking to the police. I rushed up.

"The injured girl is Alice Daly. She's been beaten and dropped on the floor by two girls. I'm worried about a head injury. I can show you the way."

I saw the principal give me a dark look. That was not something that she liked to drag the police into. She liked to handle bullying within the school. I'd never once heard her refer to a case of bullying as assault.

"Yes, please show us the way," the officer said.

I led him, his partner, and two EMTs back to the entrance. We rushed past a throng of high school students as we went down one long hall and took a left down another. A large group of kids circled around Sue and Alice.

"There," I said to the officer. "They're behind all the kids."

"Got it," he said.

He stopped at the edge of the circle.

"This is the police. You need to let us through," he said in a loud and authoritative voice. The group immediately opened up. I saw Sue and Alice right where I'd left them. The two EMTs with their kits and plastic stretcher pushed through first. They knelt down on either side of Alice. Once again, she struggled to sit up. I don't know what one EMT said, but she settled back down.

Soon they had her on the sturdy plastic stretcher with her head strapped down, as well as the rest of her, so she wouldn't fall. I figured the head strap was to keep her steady in case there was any kind of head injury.

A whole lot of chatter rose from the group of students.

Soon, Principal Sykes was telling all the students to return to their classes. After the hall cleared, the officer turned to Sue and me. "I'd like to get your statements."

"Why don't we go to my office?" Principal Sykes asked. She was all smiles for the police, but then she looked over at me, and the smile was gone. Yep, I was not her favorite person. I'd been teaching at the high school for six years. She and I had always gotten along, but this was a big boo-boo. I was in deep shit.

We all trooped along behind her, Sue and I taking up the rear.

As soon as we were all in Principal Syke's office,

which was rather large, we sat down around the table that she used for different meetings.

"First, I would like to assure you all that Alice Daly's father has been informed that his daughter is on the way to the hospital. Until we have all the information we need, we have not told him anything as to what occurred."

She looked at Sue and me and we both nodded.

The officer who had taken charge took out a notebook and smiled.

"We're here to get some facts. Who here saw what happened?"

I raised my hand. Force of schoolteacher training.

"And your name?" he asked.

"Marlowe Jones. I teach eleventh grade math."

He nodded. "Anyone else?"

"I'm the AP English teacher," Sue said.

"Did you see anything?"

"I just saw Alice on the floor and Cindy filming everything on her phone."

"Cindy?" the officer questioned. He looked around the room. I stayed silent, waiting for Principal Sykes to answer. Everyone knew Cindy, and I knew that Principal Sykes had had multiple run-ins with the girl and her parents.

Let her explain who the little wench is.

"Principal?" he prompted.

"Cindy is one of our seniors. She used to be class president until she had to step down."

"She stepped down?" the officer frowned. "Was she in trouble?"

Sykes sucked in her lips, making her look like a goldfish. "She was caught with some drugs in her locker, but she was able to explain things to our satisfaction. However, she felt compelled to step down from her presidency."

"What kind of drugs, and how much?" the second officer asked.

"It wasn't enough to sell," Sykes said.

"How much, and what?" he repeated his question.

"She had a baggie full of prescription drugs. Her parents could identify the oxycodone, and the Valium, but did not know where she might have gotten the Ritalin. But by the next day, they remembered they had an old bottle of Ritalin. That cleared everything up."

"How much?" the second officer asked again.

"I would have to ask the vice principal. He was the one who handled this."

"We'll take his statement after we've talked about this. So, Ms. Jones, what exactly did you see, and when did you see it?"

I looked down at my smart watch. "At two o'clock I left the assembly because I realized I had left my phone in my classroom. I wanted to take a video of Sharon's speech which was going to be at two-thirty. I was almost back at the assembly in seven to ten minutes, when I heard some noise around the corner. I was going to go look and see what was going on, because everybody was supposed to be at the assembly. That's when I heard a girl's voice say very loudly, 'kick her again.' Then I heard laughter. I kicked off my heels and started running down the hall."

I paused. I had been looking at the officer, but I could feel Principal Sykes' eyes on me. I glanced her way. She was staring at me. Her face was blank, but her eyes were angry.

"What did you see?" the first officer asked.

His gun belt was at my eye level. I stared at his gun for a moment, then looked upward at his badge, then at the radio on his shoulder, and then at his solemn face. He wasn't angry. He looked concerned. That was how my school's principal should have looked.

"I saw Kim Laughton literally dragging Alice Daly by her hair along the corridor, while another girl in jeans and an oversized red cardigan was kicking her in her side and back, along her kidneys and ribs."

"When I yelled out, Kim let go of Alice's hair and Alice's head hit the floor. Hard. All the time Cindy kept filming with her camera, and laughing."

"What's Cindy's last name?"

"Cindy Thompson. Her father is a state senator," I said. He didn't seem to care, but I knew Principal Sykes cared.

"Okay," he nodded. "Then what happened?"

"Sue," I pointed at Sue. "She arrived, and I told her to call 911 and help Alice. Cindy came closer and was still filming and laughing. Then she said how many likes she was going to get when she put this on the internet. That's when I demanded she give me her cell phone."

The officer nodded. "Did she give it to you?"

"Not voluntarily. I took it from her. You'll see it all on the video she took."

I reached into my skirt pocket and handed him her phone.

He handed it to the other officer.

"You can't take that. That belongs to Cindy," Principal Sykes spoke up. "Ms. Jones, you know you can't just take a phone from a student. Especially if you used force. That's what you mean when you said she didn't give the phone to you voluntarily, correct?"

I nodded.

"But Principal Sykes, Cindy intended to put everything up on the internet," Sue protested.

"It is against school policy for any teacher to lay hands on a student. You are all aware of this, it is stated in the contract that you signed."

"I did not lay hands on her. I took her cell phone away from her," I clarified.

"Forcibly?" Principal Sykes asked.

I nodded.

"Then that's a violation."

"But—" Sue started in my defense.

I interrupted her. "It's okay," I said softly.

"Ms. Jones, we will discuss this after you have finished giving your report to the police."

"Ms. Jones," the officer said. His voice just a touch

louder than Principal Sykes. "Would you be able to identify the other student if you saw her again?"

I nodded. "But you'll see her on the video."

"We have what we need for now. We're going to need your contact information in case we have more questions."

Sue and I provided them.

He looked over at Principal Sykes. "Principal Sykes, I'm surprised that a woman who likes to enforce her school policy so strictly, would not be enforcing the drug laws of this county just as diligently."

Sue looked over at me with big eyes. I tried not to laugh.

The officer continued. "I'd like to talk to you and your vice principal about the drugs you found, and any other illegal substances that you have found that you have failed to report to the proper authorities. We will have to go over every one of your reports to determine if they needed to be brought to our attention."

"Of course. I'll get him to come to my office."

I took a quick peek over at my principal and could practically see the steam rising from the top of her head. I turned to look at Sue.

"Mrs. Rankin, thank you for your quick thinking today," Principal Sykes said. "It's appreciated. Ms. Marlowe, I will need to speak to you after school today. Please return to your classes and don't discuss what happened."

We both nodded, as she picked up the telephone on her desk. We hustled out of her office.

As soon as we were past her secretary and out in the hall, Sue started talking.

"This is bullshit. The old battle axe is going to start gunning for you, and I'm not going to let her."

"Sue, keep your head down. You know how she is. Hopefully, this will blow over. Once the cops see that video, she won't have a leg to stand on."

"Like Senator Thompson will ever let that video be seen. This could turn ugly, Marlowe."

"Let's just take this one day at a time. You and I both know you can't afford to lose this job, not with Steve out of work. Don't do anything to jeopardize it. I can hold my own. If I can't, I'll move on to another school. And if push comes to shove, I'll move on to another district."

The alarm rang, indicating the end of class. Kids started pouring out of their classrooms.

Sue got close to me and whispered in my ear. "I will not let you hang out to dry."

I laughed. "I'm going to be fine. I promise. Just promise me that you'll keep your head down, all right?"

I waited until she nodded. Then I felt a tiny little bit of relief.

2

I looked at the picture of Brady and Grady, taped to the dash of my truck. One was sitting in a red wagon wearing a cowboy hat. The other was pulling the wagon, wearing red cowboy boots.

I still couldn't wrap my head around the fact that I was a twin. That my real name was Brady Beaumont and I'd been kidnapped by Arthur Beaumont when I was almost four-years-old. I'd looked at the newspaper files and Arthur Beaumont was the spitting image of Ronald Davies. So, even though I'd been kidnapped, I was still stuck claiming that son-of-a-bitch as my father. That really sucked.

Considering the fact that he hadn't one paternal instinct in the world, why in the fuck had he taken me? I mean, he couldn't put me to use on the fishing boat up in Alaska until I was ten. Of course he did have me cleaning the poor excuse of a house when I was five, and cooking for him when I was seven. At least I could do that when I wasn't resting up from some beating or another.

It got better when I started working on his fishing boat. The guys didn't like it when I was beat up, and they told him so. When five men came at dad at once to make their opinion known, Dad cut it out.

So instead of growing up in Tennessee with a mother and a brother, there was me at ten years old starting on my dad's skiff, and all those cold weeks we would spend out on the Bering Sea during crabbing season. Dad would pilot his skiff like he was Captain fucking Ahab, and me, Kenny, Lucky, Barry, Ed and Shil would take all the shit he could hand out as we'd bait the eight-hundred-pound crab traps and toss them over the side of the boat, praying that we'd get a good haul of King Crabs. Not just so the five guys would get paid, but so Ronald Davies wouldn't lose his shit.

I don't know how many prayers were said on that boat as the winch would pull up a trap, but I bet between the six of us, we prayed more than they did at St. Michaels down in Dillingham.

When crabbing season was over, he'd drop me off at Aunt Meg's every so often. She home-schooled my younger cousins. I remember badgering my aunt to tell me stories about my mom, but Aunt Meg was tightlipped. The two times I asked Dad about my mom, Dad lost his shit. Losing his shit was Dad's first gear position. Second gear was torches and pitchforks, third gear was grizzly bear mean and abusive.

As for fourth gear, you just prayed you could outrun him and hide.

Three hundred and forty-six days after I turned seventeen and got my GED I used the little money I had to buy a one-way ticket to Anchorage. Lucky had a friend of his waiting for me at the Elmendorf-Richardson base, and he took me over to the recruitment office. So I signed up then and there, to the branch that Lucky had served in.

Three years ago, I took leave from my team when Aunt Meg died. My younger cousin Sheila and I were going through her things, and that's when I found this picture. When I asked Dad about it, he acted skittish. Then he said they were kids Meg used to babysit for. When I asked him when she had lived in Tennessee, he'd lost his shit.

Of course.

He tried his normal moves, and I just smiled. I crossed my arms over my chest and stood there while he ranted and raved.

I perused my boyhood home again while I waited for him to wear himself out. The living room was a shambles. Two lamps didn't even have lampshades, just lonely lightbulbs casting light on the cheap wood paneling falling off the walls. Back when we'd lived there together, I'd done my best to keep it clean. Now the ashtrays overflowed, empty beer cans lay all over the green shag rug, and when I'd looked earlier, I'd noted that some dishes in the sink actually had mold growing in them.

I turned back to him. "Are you done?"

"Don't take that tone with me, boy. I brought you into this world, I can take you out."

Another overused Ronald Davies line.

I didn't bother to respond. "I've dreamt of this boy," I said as I pointed to the kid in the wagon. "I've dreamt of those red cowboy boots. Am I one of these kids?"

He lunged for my hand. Ronald was my height and our builds were similar, but too much beer and too many cigarettes had made him soft. Meanwhile, I trained almost every day. I'd had enough. I easily knocked him back.

"Old Man, this picture is mine. Now answer the goddamned question," I roared.

He didn't like me pushing him back. He got that shitty, shifty expression on his face. "I told you. I don't know who they are. I've never seen them before. But maybe I can find out for you."

The old man was lying through his cracked yellow teeth.

"How?"

"You know how youse always jabbering away about your mom? Well, I seem to remember her having some people in Tennessee. Maybe I can—"

A piece of wood paneling fell off the wall when I threw the old man against it. I shoved my forearm under his neck. "Don't you tell me some garbage that you think I want to hear. You fucking tell me the truth. Where is my mom?"

On my birth certificate, she was Rose McDonald. That was written in the spot for maiden name, and married name was Rose Davies. Her age was nineteen, and her place of birth was noted as Dillingham, Alaska, which was a downright lie. Not one person in this tiny little town ever heard of a Rose McDonald. I knew that. I got my hands on my birth certificate when I'd realized I wanted to join the service. I'd found it on Ronald's boat in a footlocker.

"I told you; I heard her say once that she had people in Tennessee."

"Why the lie on the birth certificate? Why did she write down she was born in Dillingham?" I demanded to know.

"She didn't know how to read or write. I put it in there. She said she was from all over down south. Her daddy had been in the Army. It was just easier to put down Dillingham."

"Where is she now?"

"Just how in the hell should I know? I told you when you was eighteen. She done robbed me blind and took off. Took all the money from one week's haul. Couldn't pay my crew."

"And why would she have done that?"

"Probably chasing after some man. She was a hussy. Took a plane right out of town. Found out she took a flight from Anchorage to Seattle. Don't know what happened to her after that."

I closed my eyes. Why did I even bother? Ronald Davies never once paid his crew fairly. It got to where Lucky would have to go with him to watch the catch being weighed and the money being paid out every time we unloaded at Dutch Harbor.

That was the last lie I allowed my father to tell me. When my leave ended, I went back to base and didn't call or write to him again. But I kept that photo in my wallet, determined that one day I would get to the bottom of this mystery.

So here I am. Pushed out of Delta Force because of a catastrophic injury that damn near caused me not to walk again. But to hear my team tell it, I had angels standing in front of me, deflecting two sniper bullets and most of the concrete shards flying all around me. My team were sure I was destined to die that night. I didn't, but it sure felt like I lost my real family, my team, when I had to leave Delta. Now, here I was tracking down a vague memory that would probably come to nothing.

I pulled off Hwy 321 toward Jasper Creek. I kept it at the speed limit; no point in tempting small town cops to rake in some additional revenue by charging me with a speeding ticket. My car navigation system told me I'd just passed over into Jasper Creek proper when I saw a sign that tickled me. It was a fifties-style waitress in a pink-and-white striped uniform, bending down at the waist holding a tray with a burger, fries, and a shake. My mouth watered. Time for some food. Maybe I could ask some questions. It was a small town. Maybe somebody would know something.

When I pulled up in my new-to-me GMC Canyon that I'd bought three days ago in Nashville, I was pleased to see that the parking lot was full. That always boded well for good food. When I got inside, the hostess said there'd be a twenty-minute wait. I didn't mind. Gave me a minute to check the news. I wanted to see what was going on in the different hot spots in the world. See where my team might be deployed.

Shit.

Fourteen aid workers had been taken in Sierra Leone. Three Americans. Last I heard, my team was now in the Middle East, and the SEAL Teams were in Africa. Still, what a clusterfuck. The aid workers had only taken four UN Peacekeepers with them.

What the hell?

I swiped over to *World of Tanks*. At least that game made sense.

"Kay, your table is ready."

"Kay, party of one, your table is ready."

I finally looked up. What with the thick Southern accent and the hostess calling out a lady's name, I didn't realize she was calling my name. I stood up and smiled down at her. She looked up at me.

"I should have remembered you," she murmured. "You're definitely all-man."

She was very pretty, and very interested, but I

33

wasn't interested in hooking up. Then there was the fact she looked like she was in high school, which did absolutely nothing for me. The only thing I was interested in was answers.

Still, I smiled. I'd learned fast in Nashville that down here; the style was friendly on steroids. Hell, just running into that Blessing lady kind of gave me a taste of the Southern way. I needed to fit in, so smiling needed to be my go-to. Up in Alaska, your neighbor wasn't just your neighbor, they were your lifeline. But this smiling and treating everybody like your friend thing, wasn't how I grew up. Add my father into the mix, and this was pretty damned foreign. I might have been stationed in North Carolina, but I was mostly out of the country.

"You said you were good to sit up at the counter, right?"

I nodded.

"I have a spot between the sheriff and Harvey."

I almost laughed. She said that like I should know who those two men were. "Sounds good," I muttered.

"Menus are at the counter. Don't forget to get yourself a piece of pie. The peaches, pears and apples are grown at Millie's." She pointed to an empty seat at the counter, and I made my way there.

The man who looked up when I sat down was eating a salad. The one who kept eating had a mountain of a meal in front of him. I had no idea what it was, except it was covered in gravy. The salad-eater nodded to me as I grabbed a menu. Then he went back to his salad. I'd had the menu in my hand for less than a minute when a middle-aged woman with a beehive hairdo and bright red lipstick stepped in front of me.

"Coffee?" she asked as she held a pot.

"Yes, ma'am."

She flipped over the ceramic mug and poured like she'd been doing it for years. "Are you Pearl?" I asked.

"The one and only," she said proudly. "Pearl Bannister. What's your name?"

"Kai Davies."

"Pleased to meet you, Kai Davies. Your name doesn't sound familiar, but your face is. Have you been through Jasper Creek before?"

I could feel the salad-eater listening to our conversation. I thought he must be the sheriff.

"Nope, this is my first time in Tennessee. My dad told me I might have relatives around here on my mother's side. I thought I would check that out."

"What's her name?"

"Rose McDonald."

"Doesn't sound familiar." She turned to the salad-eater. "What about you, Nash? Do you know any McDonalds with a girl named Rose who'd be old enough to have birthed Kai?"

Nash looked up, his lip twitching. "Can't say that I do."

Pearl shrugged her shoulders. "Sorry, son. Doesn't sound like we can be of much help. You might want to talk to Little Grandma. She's older

35

than dirt. Knows everybody. She might be able to help you."

"Where can I find her?"

"Down Home Café. You can't miss it. It's right on the town square. She works the breakfast and lunch shifts."

"Thank you." I smiled.

"I'll leave you to study the menu." She smiled back at me.

"You don't have to leave. The sign outside decided me. I'll take a bacon cheeseburger, rare, with American cheese and grilled onions, strawberry shake, and fries. Apparently, I'm supposed to order pie for dessert."

Nash spoke up. "That's mandatory."

The guy to my left stopped shoveling his food for a moment. "You can never go wrong with pie."

"I'm sold."

"Your food will be right up," Pearl promised.

3

"Well, Chaos are you going to be at home here? I know the yard isn't as big as the one in West Virginia, but it was all I could find to rent on such short notice." Not to mention within my budget. My savings had already taken enough of a hit, so a manageable rent was a major factor when finding a place here in Jasper Creek.

Chaos looked up at me and tilted her head.

"Exactly. The red front porch swing makes up for everything. I agree."

My big Bernese Mountain dog followed me out of the bedroom and into the kitchen, which was still a mess. I had boxes everywhere. I so should have unpacked the kitchen before I unpacked the bedroom.

"No cooked food for you tonight, sweetie. It's Alpo and kibble for din-din."

She whined. My baby totally understood me.

"I know, I know, I'm not too happy either. The store's closed and all I get is another protein bar and Gatorade."

This time, she really whined.

I bent down and gave her a deep rub, concentrating on her neck and shoulders. Her tail wagged.

"And I hate to tell you, I'm too tired to take you for a walk. You're going to have to take a spin around the backyard by yourself."

She whined again.

No question about it. Chaos understood what I was saying. Being named after such a complex theory like the Chaos Theory, of course she would understand. I liked the idea that she represented the process that nothing could ever be predicted, and considering how my life was turning out, that sure as hell was the truth. Plus, she often stirred up chaos in my life, and I loved her for that.

I rubbed on her some more.

"You like that, don't you?"

Chaos pressed her cold nose against my neck.

"Don't worry, girl, the grocery store is top of the list tomorrow morning, and I'll be well rested so we can explore the neighborhood. I'll get us fed right now, then we can unpack the kitchen and hit the sack. What do you think about that?"

She yawned.

"Hey, don't get me started. We still have a couple of hours left to go."

I dug her food and bowls out of the duffle bag

that I'd made up for her before we'd left this morning from the house Granny had left me in Madison. I'd snagged a can opener and soon had her dinner ready.

I hated leaving Granny's house. But at least I didn't have to sell it. Maybe one day I could go back home to Madison, but for now, my job was here in Jasper Creek. Who knew, maybe Sue's husband would actually get a bite and my old house would actually get rented, and I'd have a little bit of extra money in my pocket.

Yay me.

Chaos came over to the bowl, sniffed, and walked away. I shrugged. She'd eventually eat when she got hungry enough. I grabbed the protein bar and warm Gatorade out of my oversized purse and forced it down, then got to work unpacking boxes. Every so often, I would run another load of laundry that I hadn't finished before I'd left West Virginia.

Beau hadn't been kidding when he said that the kitchen had been updated. Even these appliances were top of the line. It was a wonder that he wasn't charging me more. He told me he'd worked a deal with the contractor, but still…

It took me three and a half hours to get everything unpacked and put away or put into the dishwasher. There was no way I was going to eat on the dishes after they had been packed away in newspaper.

I looked over when I heard Chaos' claws on the

wood floor. She went for her bowl of food. She took another sniff and then looked at me and whined.

"Look here, my mathematical theory, don't turn all high and mighty. Be a heroine and suck it up. You'll get good food tomorrow."

I laughed when she started eating the Alpo.

Now that I was done with all the dirty work, I needed a shower and a glass of wine. I washed out one of the wineglasses, then realized I didn't have any wine.

"Dammit!"

Well, this was not a good way to start my new life. I should have bought wine to celebrate. After all, this was a new chapter.

Well, at least I'd get a good night's sleep.

Everything about this house was old and beautiful. I loved the original hardwood floors. I'd never seen this type of wood before. I'd have to research on the internet what kind of wood it was. I yawned so hard as I was walking down the hall to the main bedroom that I seriously considered foregoing the shower. Then I saw my bed all made up with yellow sheets and the yellow duvet with sunflowers, and I couldn't bring myself to go to bed dirty, so I headed for the shower.

The warm water almost put me to sleep standing up, but I managed to get out and dry myself. My hair was useless. Thick and blonde, there was no way I was going to try to dry it tonight, so I just braided it and headed for bed.

I was almost asleep when the bed shook and Chaos made herself comfortable against my back. She was a cuddler. Then I fell into a deep, dreamless sleep.

I heard a thud that woke me up. Chaos had hit the floor. I rubbed my eyes and noted the sun shimmering through the gauzy curtains. I grinned. I couldn't imagine Beau being the delicate curtain kind of guy. Maybe it was the last tenant. He'd said he hadn't stepped foot in the house in over fifteen years. He had an old friend named Bernie Faulkes, who checked up on things. Beau said he was quite the character and I might want to go introduce myself.

It had been fun talking to Beau. He'd explained to me that I was looking to rent at the perfect time, because this way I could actually talk to him instead of Bernie. Normally he wouldn't have the time to FaceTime, but his team had some downtime. I made the mistake of asking some questions, like where he was and what he was doing, and what branch of the service he was in. All I got out of him was he was a Marine in Europe. He didn't seem mad that I had asked questions, probably because I didn't push, I just moved onto other things.

Beau was really serious. I couldn't get him to crack a smile on any of the three FaceTime calls we had. The only time he came close was when he mentioned getting a piece of pie at Pearl's. He told me to skip the apple and go for the peach. When he mentioned he hadn't stepped foot in the house for fifteen years, it took me a moment to think of something to say to that. Finally, I went with the obvious, "Why?"

"Don't get me wrong. Jasper Creek is a friendly town, but it was time for me to leave."

I figured I could circle back to that on our fourth FaceTime call, but that never happened. Instead, I got a call from Bernie Faulkes to complete the paperwork on renting the house. When I asked about Beau, Bernie just said that Marine Raiders were always called away at a moment's notice.

With one last glance at the curtains, I rolled out of bed. Since Chaos was already up, I knew she needed to take a walk for her morning business. I headed to the bathroom and did my thing, then hit the small closet that *almost* fit my clothes. I pulled out my wide-leg jeans, the red belt with the gold Wonder Woman buckle, and the almost-pink crop top that Sue had got me. After I had that on, I grabbed one of my favorite slouchy sweaters—cream with pink hearts—and slipped on my Vans Old Skool sneakers.

"Chaos, we're going for a walk!"

I headed to the kitchen and grabbed some poop bags and her leash. I saw her empty bowls.

"Food first?"

She headed to the front door.

"I guess that answers that." I grinned.

I jogged down the stairs, and off we went down the street. Dogwood was a beautiful street. It had gorgeous old maple and oak trees planted on either side of the street. I grinned when I saw that almost every yard had a dogwood tree planted in it. It seemed like nobody could handle living on a street called Dogwood and not having a dogwood tree in their front yard.

"Hey there, Missy. Are you enjoying the sunshine?"

I stopped short. I couldn't find who was talking to me. I finally spotted a woman who was on her porch across the street watering her ferns.

"Yes, ma'am. I am."

"You must be the new schoolteacher, am I right?"

"Yes, ma'am. I am."

"Well, come on over. I have fresh coffee cake. You can even bring that behemoth of a dog with you. My cat ain't scared of dogs."

"My name is Marlowe Jones," I said as I crossed the street. Chaos was actually leading me at this point. She knew when she'd spotted a friend.

"I know your name is Marlowe Jones. A lot of us were at the school board meeting where they voted whether or not to hire you. You sure got a raw deal at that prissy school, but we all liked your spunk. It was an easy vote, it ended up being unanimous."

I winced. I'd had no choice but to use Sue as my reference. It sounds like she made me sound better than I was.

She motioned me to join her on the porch. "Well, that's real nice, Mizz...?"

"Lettie Magill. I was born and raised here in Jasper Creek. Followed my husband for his job for a few years when he moved to Dallas, but we came back after six years. So, I know the lay of the land. You come on in, and I'll tell you what to expect at the school."

She was a lot to take in, but she seemed sincere. "Can I come over after Chaos is done with her morning constitutional?"

Lettie laughed. "I would prefer it. If I hadn't seen your resume, and listened to your accent, I would think with that big fancy word, that you were a Northerner."

"Nope, I bleed country," I laughed.

"Well, come on back. If I don't answer when you knock, just let yourself in. The doorbell is busted. I'll probably have my fancy standing mixer on and can't hear you knock."

Only in the South.

"Okay, I shouldn't be more than a half hour. And I can certainly leave Chaos at my house," I offered.

"Nonsense. Icicle needs someone to play with."

I grinned. "Okay, Lettie. I'll be back in a half hour or so. Thank you for the invitation."

Lettie looked up from her Kitchen Aid mixer. "Glad you made it," she said as she turned it off. "Sit yourself down." She indicated the little nineteen-seventies dinette with the orange vinyl covering on it that was set in the kitchen.

"I set out some food for your dog. What is his name again?"

"Her name is Chaos." I told her. I was charmed that she thought of putting out some food for my dog. "You had dog food?"

"I had some left-over brisket and gravy and threw it into my food processor."

"Lettie, that was extremely kind of you." I was still holding onto her leash when Chaos spotted the bowl with the food. She sat down and looked back at me.

"Well, aren't you polite?" Lettie smiled. "Go ahead, dig in."

I nodded at Chaos and unhooked her leash. I watched as she walked calmly to the dish. Not her normal rampage toward food. Then her ladylike manners went down the drain as she shoved her muzzle into the bowl and started chowing down.

Lettie and I laughed.

"Now for us."

She pulled open the oven door, and the heavenly smell of coffeecake wafted through the kitchen. My stomach grumbled. I guess neither of the Jones girls were behaving ladylike this morning.

"I hope you like this. I've also put together fruit cups. A friend of mine has an orchard, and she always

45

sends me home with fresh peaches and pears, when they're in season. What would you like to drink? Coffee? Juice? Milk?"

"I would kill for a cup of coffee. Chaos needed to be taken on a walk before I had a chance to make a pot."

Chaos lifted her head up when she heard her name. I smiled and shook my head. She went back to eating.

Soon I had the necessary caffeine in my system and a feast in front of me. I liked Lettie's style. There was no little dainty piece of cake. She gave me a healthy slice, *and* she brought butter. She was my kind of woman.

"Did you get a chance to talk to Beau when you rented his place?" Lettie asked.

I nodded my head and swallowed my bite of pear.

"Yeah, we FaceTimed for a few days. I got the feeling he was kind of lonely for conversation that wasn't military related."

Lettie leaned forward. "How was he doing? Did he seem in good spirits?"

I frowned. "What do you mean, exactly?"

Lettie paused and took a sip of her coffee. "Beau left Jasper Creek fifteen years ago. As soon as he turned eighteen, he signed up for the military. He became a Marine. He hasn't been back since."

I tried to process what she *wasn't* saying, but I wasn't getting her subtext. My confusion must have shown on my face, because Lettie continued.

"Beau had a hard childhood. His dad was mean. When I say mean. I'm serious. He should have been locked up, considering how many times the sheriff was called to their house, but he and the sheriff were tight. Nothing ever came of all the calls. I wasn't living here at the time, but I heard about things."

I could imagine. There had been two times I had to call CPS on behalf of one of my students. It was yet another black mark on my record as far as Principal Sykes was concerned. But my parents had instilled a bedrock knowledge of right and wrong that had never once wavered.

"So, what happened?" I asked.

"Finally, Beau ended up in the hospital. They didn't know if he was going to live or die. His daddy had kicked him so bad in the side with his steel-toed boot, he cut him open and one of his ribs punctured his lungs. Brady saw the whole thing."

"Who's Brady?"

"Beau's twin brother. The boys weren't yet four years old."

"He did that to a four-year-old?" Images of a chubby baby's broken body flashed before my eyes and it took everything I had not to cry. "How can a monster like that be possible?"

"His mama told the sheriff that Beau had spilled Arthur's beer."

"He seemed all right when I talked to him. How long did it take for him to recover?" I asked her.

"Months. But it was like Rose and Beau lost their

way when Beau came home. Arthur was gone, and so was Brady. The sheriff said he notified everyone and even brought in the FBI, but Brady was never found."

"That's outrageous! If he would do that to Beau, imagine what he's doing or did to Brady."

"We all did. His mother, Rose, was never the same. Neither was Beau. Most of the town put it down to his injuries, but not my granny. Little Grandma was sure that he was missing his other half."

I couldn't eat another bite. Even now, what I had eaten felt like lead in my stomach.

"I can tell you he seemed good when I talked to him. I did wonder why he was renting out his house, sight unseen. He'd told me he hadn't stepped foot in it for over fifteen years, which seemed odd."

"What seems odd is that he hasn't sold it." Lettie stood up and took our plates to the sink. She scraped off the uneaten coffee cake into the garbage.

"What happened to his mother?"

"She died six months before he joined the service. Everybody knew she just didn't have the will to live. She'd been a shadow of herself for years. She'd just been holding on for Beau."

"Living with a depressed mama must have been hard for him." Chaos came and laid her head on my thigh, and I petted her head.

Lettie nodded as she sat back down. "He was a good boy. He took care of her. The ladies in the community did what they could, but most of the burden fell on Beau."

My heart ached for the young man who had been beaten so badly and lost his brother. Then to care for his mother? It was unthinkable.

"Wasn't there any family?"

"Rose came from some family up North. Minnesota. Social Services contacted her parents, but they wanted nothing to do with her. Eventually the social worker found out that Rose had been told if she married Arthur, she'd be disowned. They didn't care about her current circumstances. I know that hit our community hard. Who could be that cold?"

I shook my head. The sad part was, I could see it. Teaching in the public school system for six years had opened my eyes to a lot of things. But this had to be one of the saddest stories I'd ever heard.

Lettie continued. "By the time Beau was ten, me, Robert and our daughters had moved back. I know my Little Grandma and my mama had tried to help, but Rose and Beau would only allow so much. Thank God he got into sports. It opened him up some. He had something more than just his mother in his life." She leaned forward. "But for sure he sounded good?" she asked again.

I smiled and patted her hand. "Yes. He smiled and talked. Lettie, I promise you, he even laughed."

She sat back in her chair. "I can't tell you how happy that makes me. Wait until I tell my mama and Little Grandma. That'll make their week." She grinned at me. "Scratch that. It'll make their month."

"I really have to go. We don't have anything in the

house to eat. I like to cook, so I want to make a trip to the grocery store. Maybe I can invite you and your husband over to my house for dinner next week. How does that sound?"

"That sounds lovely."

By the time I was walking down her porch steps, I could swear I heard her on the phone. I would bet anything she was calling her mama or grandmother to tell them about Beau.

4

There wasn't a lot to choose from when it came to a place to crash. I could pay an exorbitant rate at the Whispering Pines Inn or I could stay at the LeeHy motel. I chose the LeeHy motel. It was on the outskirts of Jasper Creek, next to the trailer park. When I passed Blue Ash Village Trailer Park, it didn't look so bad. Especially compared to some of the refugee camps I'd seen in the Middle East and Africa.

I pulled into the LeeHy and found a young kid behind the reception desk picking his nose with one hand and swiping left with his other hand. He looked to be about fourteen, by the way he slouched behind the counter and didn't bother to look up when I came in through the door.

"I'd like to book a room," I said.

"Yeah, by the hour or by the night?" At least he stopped mining for nose nuggets. Instead, he used two hands to handle his phone.

"By the night. I don't know how long I'll be, at least three nights."

"I'm going to need a major credit card, but there's a discount if you pay in cash." He *did* look up at me when he mentioned cash.

I was pretty sure I knew whose pocket the cash would go into. I really didn't want him to get rewarded for doing nothing, but I didn't want him touching my card. Plus, I thought it was highly likely he'd be selling my credit card info to a buddy before the night was over.

"How much?"

He told me, and I slid the exact amount over to him.

The kid gave me a shifty look.

"If you want towels, that's going to be extra."

Lovely.

"How much?"

"Six dollars."

I only had twenties. I spied the towels behind him on a shelf. I walked behind the desk and pulled a pile of towels and gave him a twenty.

"How much for a clean room?"

He gave me a confused look, and I sighed.

The Whispering Pines Inn was sounding better and better.

He handed over the card key for the room, which I had no choice but to take from him. I knew I'd dealt with far worse in the field, but goddammit, I was in America. I really didn't think I should have to put up with this crap. I wiped the card off on one of the towels and handed the towel back to him. He started to say something, but my expression stopped him.

Good.

I picked up my extremely light duffel bag and hitched up my backpack as I tuned out his explanation of how I would find room 201. I was already figuring out my next move for tomorrow. First thing? Figure out where Grady Beaumont lived. But I needed a clear head before I found my potential brother.

When I opened the door to my room, I sighed. It was a shambles. I walked back down to visit with Derek. Eventually he figured out that room 205 had been cleaned, so he gave me that key. I got more towels, wiped off the key card again, and left the hand towel with him.

As I walked to the room, I figured I had a fifty-fifty chance of him being right about the room being clean. I sure as hell hoped he was, because my shoulder was killing me and I needed to take something for the pain.

I was pleasantly surprised when I opened the door and found a clean room that even smelled nice. I saw that there was a fresh carnation in a vase on the small table in the corner of the room. Somebody obviously took their job seriously. I was impressed.

I locked the door, then saw that the chain lock was busted and sighed. Of course it was busted. I dumped my duffel and backpack on the second double bed and headed for the shower and was soon happily under a hot spray with better water pressure than I'd expected.

After I got done, I put on a fresh set of clothes and booted up my laptop. It was one of the few things that had kept me sane at Walter Reed.

I pulled up my file on Brady and Grady Beaumont of Jasper Creek. Sons of Rose and Arthur Beaumont. I'd found Rose's death certificate. She'd died twelve years ago. Her maiden name was McBride. I didn't find any current information on Arthur or Brady, but Grady enlisted in the Marines when he was eighteen. He was currently serving as a Marine Raider.

So he was in Special Operations. Didn't that sound familiar?

Seemed like I needed to talk to Little Grandma. Since I had to wait until morning, I might as well shoot the shit with Clay if he was in country.

I went to the bed and piled up all the pillows behind my back and shoulders and pressed in Clay's number.

"So, you remembered me after all? What took you so long? I've only left eight voicemails and texted you eighteen times."

"Don't you have some woman to stalk instead?" I asked.

"Nah, the two I had my eye on took out restraining orders."

I laughed. "Seriously, you should start dating."

"Who in the hell wants to date a Spec Op when

54

we never know when we're leaving or for how long, and we can never tell our woman shit?"

"Rick's wife. Brandon's fiancé. To name two."

"Yeah, well, they're both something special. Trying to find somebody else like them is impossible."

Behind Clay's nonchalance, I heard just a little bit of pain. I knew he wanted what his parents and siblings had. At the same time, he didn't want to leave the teams.

"Anyway, I wasn't leaving you messages to discuss my love life. I was tracking you down to see how you were doing, and if you're still trying to find out if you're not related to that fucking prick, Ronald."

"Yes and yes."

"Care to elaborate?"

"Not really. How is everybody?"

"I'll let you deflect my question for three minutes. That's all."

"You're a pain in my ass," I told my best friend.

He laughed.

"They're all real good. Frank took his test and got promoted to an E-5. He's pretty damn happy. Rice is pretty sure he saw him dancing outside the cafeteria when he found out."

I laughed. "That's great. He can use the extra pay now that he and Julie have a baby on the way."

"Dude, you're so behind the times. The baby's name is Andrea, and she's five months old. Frank told me he sent you a picture."

"There were two other guys named Davis at Walter Reed. They kept getting our names mixed up and our mail mixed up, even though my name is Davies. Mike said he would forward my mail as soon as I gave him a permanent or semi-permanent address."

"Mike?"

"Mike Kowalski, my demon from hell physical therapist. He was the best of the bunch. Used to be a submariner during his four years in the Navy. Came out and got his college degree and played football. Was scouted by the Philadelphia Eagles. Third year as linebacker, he got knocked sideways in his knees. Did a year in physical therapy, played another two years and was injured again, and that was all she wrote. He went back to school for his Doctor of Physical Therapy and has been at Walter Reed ever since."

"Quite a story."

"Yeah. I hated and loved him at the same time."

"You would have loved him more if he got you back to our team."

"The docs were straight with me. That wasn't going to happen. I was lucky that I ended up with full range of motion."

Clay sucked in a deep breath. "Shit."

"Yep, that sums it up."

We were silent for a long moment.

"So, a baby girl, huh?" I finally said.

"Yeah, looks just like Julie. Frank is going to be in

so much trouble when she turns sixteen. He better keep his gun handy."

"What about the rest of the gang? How are they doing?"

In the eleven years I'd been with this team, we'd had men transfer out, we'd had men retire, two were injured, but they'd come back. Eight years ago, Sully died, but it hadn't been in the field. So the core group of us, Clay, me, Lisbon, Zypher, John and Ramsey, had held strong. Other Raider teams talked about us. But then that day when the bullet hit the cement, fragments hit me, our luck had run out again. Clay knew who I wanted to know about.

"Zephyr is still hung up on the girl he met in Canada when we went heli-skiing in the Canadian Rockies."

I smiled. That had been one of our best two-week leaves.

"I sure as hell won't be doing that for a while," I sighed.

"What did your demon from hell say about that?"

"Hell, Clay. I'm still not supposed to lift anything over twenty-five pounds. The demon told me that if I do my exercises religiously, I could graduate up to forty pounds in another four weeks."

"So? Do your exercises religiously. In the meantime, we'll just change our plans and do the sand boarding in Namibia next year. The only lifting required will be your snowboard. Just don't land on your bad shoulder. Easy as pie."

"You know. That doesn't sound too bad. As a matter of fact, that sounds damn good."

"Well, keep doing what the football god tells you to do."

I laughed again. Talking to Clay was just the medicine I needed.

"Okay, that was enough deflection. Tell me how the hunt is going."

"I'm in Jasper Creek. So far, nothing. I was told that there might be somebody who could tell me something. A woman who owns a diner told me that there is this other woman who is, and I'm quoting, old as dirt, and she would remember Rose McDonald and the twins. Maybe even their father, Arthur Beaumont. I won't be able to get in touch with her until tomorrow morning."

"So, you really didn't want to talk to me. You were just bored. Is that it?"

I laughed yet again. "That about sums it up."

Clay laughed too. "Well, get bored more often. I worry about you."

I shut my eyes for a moment. Clay was my brother, and I'd been out of line shutting him out. "I promise."

"Thank God. Now give me your address. My mom wants to send you some cookies."

"I haven't landed anyplace yet," I admitted.

"You're sleeping somewhere tonight, aren't you?"

"In a motel, that really should be called a Motel 3."

"That bad?"

"Except for the fresh flower in the room. I had to pay extra for the towels, and I didn't trust the nose-picker desk clerk far enough to give him my credit card. First, I didn't want him touching it. Second, I worried if he had it on file, he'd use it."

"Sounds like you found a winner."

"Sure did. I'll be changing tomorrow night."

"Call me when you get the address."

"I doubt I'll be staying that long."

"Where else do you have to be?"

Now wasn't that the question of the year?

5

At seven o'clock sharp, I was out of the motel and at the Down Home Diner. It was already open, and half the tables were full. My stomach started rumbling as soon as the smells hit me. There was bacon and coffee, that was for sure, but there were other things that had me almost salivating. The protein bar I'd had at four o'clock that morning wasn't cutting it.

I walked up to the hostess station and grinned. The little old lady sitting on the stool beside the station grinned back at me, then she frowned.

"Wait just a dog-gone minute. Is that you, Beau?"

I tilted my head and looked at her. My heart beat a little faster. "Beau?"

"Don't be giving me any of your sass, boy. I might be old. Real old, but my eyesight is just fine." She gave me a mischievous grin. "Well, good for a girl one-hundred-and-one years young. Now you answer me,

Grady Beau Beaumont. Have you finally decided to come home? Because it's about dang time."

"Ma'am, my name isn't Beau. My name is Kai Davies. To my knowledge, I've lived up in Alaska my entire life, but I found this photo in my aunt's possessions after she passed." I pulled out my wallet and handed her the photo that said Grady and Brady, Jasper Tennessee.

She sucked in a loud breath as she looked down at the picture.

"Little Grandma, are you going to let us in, or what? We're hungry."

I turned around to see five people standing behind me. One man looked very impatient, and I recognized him from yesterday afternoon at Pearl's. He was the gravy guy.

"Hold your horses, Harvey. This is important." Little Grandma waved her hand at him.

She looked down at the picture in her hand, then looked back up at me. "Kai Davies, Brady Beaumont disappeared almost thirty years ago. So did his daddy, Arthur. Arthur was a mean sumbitch. We never did know what happened to him, or that little boy. Beau joined the Marines when he turned eighteen. He came back a few times to sort out his mama's things and start renting out his house on Dogwood. After that we ain't never seen hide nor hair of him again. That's been nigh on fourteen years. You're the spitting image of Beau."

"Little Grandma," Harvey growled.

"Lettie," Little Grandma hollered out. "Come seat Harvey before he gnaws a leg off a chair. Then seat the others. Will you, Darlin'?"

A pretty, curvy, middle-aged woman came over and plucked some menus out of Little Grandma's hand and glowered at Harvey. "This way, you overgrown horse's behind. Just for causing trouble, you're not getting a cinnamon roll with your meal."

"Lettie, that's just not fair," I heard him whine as she took him to a table near the back of the restaurant.

Little Grandma looked up at the others. "Here's the menus. The rest of you can seat yourselves. You'll get a free cinnamon roll with your meals today for waiting so patiently, so eat hearty."

I was in a daze as I watched her customers thank her profusely, take the menus, and go into the dining room. All I could really think about, all I could really concentrate on, was that I had a brother. And his name was Beau.

"What's your daddy's name?" Little Grandma asked.

"Ronald. Ronald Davies. His sister's name was Sheila. She died three years ago."

"That's a shame, son. I'll say a prayer for her. Do you have a picture of your daddy?"

I shook my head. There was never a reason to take a picture of Ronald. Never.

"Well, welcome home, Brady Beaumont."

She reached up and enveloped me in a hug that

smelled like cinnamon and roses. I found myself hugging her back. When she released me, it was like my entire world had turned upside down.

I have a brother.

My name was Brady Beaumont.

I have a brother.

The woman in front of me seemed to understand.

"Lettie," she called out.

Lettie finished up pouring cups of coffee for a table, then rushed over. "Yes'm?"

"Clear off that table in the corner. Get this boy a full breakfast. And I mean everything."

"French toast, or pancakes?" she asked.

"Both. I don't know what he likes, but I want him to have a choice."

Lettie headed for the table.

"Make sure he gets a cinnamon roll too," Little Grandma called over her shoulder as she slowly got off her chair and then pulled me toward the table in the corner in front of the window. Lettie led the way and started clearing the table.

"Little Grandma, why does he get a cinnamon roll and I don't?" Harvey whined again.

"Your wife told me that your sugar is high. Plus, you were rude. You're lucky you're getting syrup, so hush up."

My lip kicked up. Even in Dillingham, which was a much smaller burg than this place, people weren't this deep into one another's business.

"It's clean. What do you want, Little Grandma?" Lettie asked as she stood up straight.

"Tea and a biscuit with honey. No butter."

"I'll have your orders up in a jiffy. Do you want coffee?" she asked me.

I nodded. She turned over the coffee mug on the table and poured me a cup.

I looked around the diner and saw a few people looking over at us. They were definitely curious about what was going on. Apparently, it wasn't often that Little Grandma sat down with a customer.

"You have questions, don't you? Go ahead and ask."

It took me a minute. All of my brain cells were firing at once. I took a deep breath, then another. Just as if I had a target in sight as I was holding my sniper rifle. I nodded at the old woman in front of me.

"I found Rose Beaumont's death certificate. It said her maiden name was McBride. My dad always said my mother's maiden name was McDonald."

"Arthur was an asshole. Pardon my French."

"The death certificate said she died of cancer. Did she suffer long?"

"Six months before Beau graduated from high school. She was in a bad way. She'd been depressed for a long time. It was hard on Beau. All of us tried to help her. Get her professional help, but she refused. She clung to Beau and then, when she got the cancer, he nursed her. Again, all of us tried to pitch in, but

64

she didn't want us around, and he said he could handle it."

"When was she diagnosed with cancer?"

"When Beau was fifteen. For the last five months of her life, she refused treatment. Just stayed at home and forced Beau to take care of her. But me and some of the other ladies in town forced our way into the situation so that Beau didn't miss school. It would have been a shame if he hadn't been able to graduate."

"So that's why Beau never comes back to Jasper Creek."

She nodded. "I hear tell he's busy climbing mountains and such when he does take leave. He keeps in touch with Bernie Falks. Bernie usually takes care of the whole renting process for Beau since he owns the house free and clear, but since Bernie married Mora, he hasn't had time to do it for him. I heard tell that Beau took care of the renting by the internet."

Climbing mountains and such?

"Besides climbing mountains, do you know what else he does?"

"Jumping on a base or something. Lettie's daughter might know. She was all excited about it when she heard about it."

Jumping on a base?

"Could it be base jumping?" I asked.

"Maybe. You'll have to ask Theresa. She doesn't come over until after her classes, about two o'clock. She helps to clean up and do prep work for the next day."

"Okay." I grinned. Seemed like I had a lot in common with my brother. I needed to get in touch with this Bernie Faulkes character to see if he could arrange for me to FaceTime with Beau. I was anxious to see my old house, too. Maybe it would spark some memories.

"Besides joining the Marines, renting his house, and base jumping, do you know anything else? Has he ever married? Does he have a girlfriend? Kids?"

"I'm sorry, son. I don't know anything like that. It's best that you talk to Bernie. Let me have someone give you—"

"Order up!"

Four plates were put in front of me. One had waffles with strawberries and whipped cream. One had French toast with a side of something. Another had a stack of at least five pancakes. The main plate had biscuits and gravy, some eggs with cheese, peppers, and tomatoes. There were grits and home fries. If I had come off a mission, I could do justice to this breakfast, but coming out of the hospital, I just couldn't.

"I'll be right back with your tea and biscuit, Little Grandma," Lettie said in a loving voice.

"Don't forget Brady's cinnamon roll."

"I wanted to get him a fresh one. Mom's icing it right now."

"Good thinking." Little Grandma smiled.

My stomach growled. Well, maybe I might be able

to put a dent in the food. Not the waffles, though. All the whipped cream just seemed too much like dessert for breakfast, but I'd make an exception for the cinnamon roll.

Because.

Well.

Cinnamon roll.

I started to dig in, thinking about what I wanted to do besides contacting Bernie. Then it came to me. I wanted to see the porch that was always in my dreams. The porch where there had been a red swing.

"I have Beau's address in my navigation system. I can just drive by after breakfast." I said after I had swallowed a big forkful of liberally buttered grits.

"Do those actually work?" Little Grandma frowned. "In case they don't, take First Street out of the town square. After the railroad tracks, you'll start hitting the tree streets. Dogwood is after Maple. If you've made it to Ash, you've gone too far."

She poured a little bit of milk into her tea and stirred. Then took a tiny sip and smiled. She nodded at my plate of pancakes. "You better start in on them before they get cold. Nothing worse than cold pancakes."

"Yes'm."

I continued to eat my food.

"Lettie?" Little Grandma called out.

Lettie hustled over and smiled. "Is everything okay?"

I nodded because my mouth was full.

Little Grandma spoke. "Everything is fine. Why don't you call Sherray in to cover your shift? Brady here wants to look at his old family home. You live on Dogwood, you could guide him to the old Beaumont place."

"I was just talking to the gal who rented the house. I'd be glad to take you. Let me get Sherray in here to cover my shift, then you can follow me." She looked down at the table. "I'll also get you another cup of coffee."

I nodded because my mouth was full again.

Seriously, did they add crack to this food?

Little Grandma didn't say anything while I continued to eat. She looked out the window and occasionally smiled and dipped her head at someone who passed by, but mostly she just sat there, contentedly sipping her tea and nibbling on her biscuit. After I finished all of my French toast, three of my pancakes, and almost everything on my main plate, I looked up at her and shook my head. "I can't believe I ate that much."

"Where are you staying?"

"The LeeHy motel."

"I do hope you didn't check in last night. Young Derek works nights, and despite coming from a wonderful family, he just came out wrong. All of his brothers and sisters are upstanding citizens, but young Derek is the bane of Roger and Harmony's existence."

"Yeah, I met him."

"You might want to think about changing venues."

"You've read my mind."

6

"Nice rig." Lettie smiled. "My husband would approve."

"He likes GMCs?"

"He has a Chevy truck, so yeah." Her smile grew wider. She got into the passenger seat of my truck, not needing any help. She'd explained that she drove in with her mother and her husband picked her up from work.

I closed the passenger door, then got into the driver's seat and followed her directions to her house. I wished I could say that the streets seemed familiar, but they didn't.

"Take a right at the next stop sign," Lettie said. "Then we're going to go five blocks."

"Sounds easy enough." I grimaced as I saw all the pink and white dogwood blossoms. My stomach started getting tight. Jesus, did every single house have to have a dogwood tree?

"You okay?" Lettie asked. Her voice was soft. Like she was talking to a girl. A child.

"Fine, ma'am."

"Lettie," she corrected me.

I nodded. I couldn't get a word out, my teeth were clamped closed.

As we got closer and closer, I went slower and slower, until I was only going ten miles an hour as we passed the last stop sign.

"There it is, on the left. Do you recognize it?"

I looked out my window, and I shook my head, then nodded. There was the porch and the four steps. But there wasn't dirt at the bottom. There was a walkway lined with purple flowers, but I lurched to a stop when I saw the red porch swing.

"Brady, are you all right?"

Again, she was talking to me like I was fragile. Same way they'd talked to me after I'd come out of my coma at Walter Reed. I was a Green Beret, I wasn't fucking fragile.

"Brady?"

"My name is Kai. I'm fine, ma'am." I stopped staring at the swing. "I mean, Lettie. I'm fine, Lettie."

"This is your old house, isn't it?"

I nodded. My jaw hurt. I opened my mouth, releasing my bite.

"Your brother is going to be mighty glad to see you," she whispered.

Lettie was a nice enough lady, but I'd had enough.

I looked at her and forced a smile. "Where can I drop you off?"

Again, she gave me that smile, as if she knew what I was feeling. She didn't. She couldn't.

She pointed to a house with a riot of roses and some other enormous flower on the corner. "I know the woman who's renting the house. Would you like me to introduce you?"

I looked back over at the red porch swing. It was as I remembered it, only a lot smaller. Which made sense, since I'd been almost four years old when I'd been taken away by dear old dad.

"Kai?"

"What?" *Oh yeah. Introduce.* "Maybe later. I need to check out of the LeeHy Motel and check-in to the Whispering Pines Inn."

"Oh, let me call on over to Gretchen. She's managing things at Whisper these days. I'll let her know you're coming. Do you know where it is?"

"I'll put the name into my phone and take it from there." I knew I wasn't paying attention and when I looked over at the woman, I saw that she could tell I wasn't too. "Let me get you to your house."

"All right. I don't suppose I could invite you in for some homemade lemonade and apple brown betty?"

"I'm stuffed," I said as I eased up to her house. Before I had a chance to turn off the engine, Lettie had her seatbelt off and the passenger door open. Then she stopped and looked at me. "You come back to the diner, you hear? It'll make Little Grandma happy. Also, stop by my place anytime you want me to introduce you to Marlowe. I get off at three every day, and Marlowe doesn't start work until the third week of August. She's a teacher."

"Who's Marlowe again?"

"She's the woman renting your old house. Plus, she's the one who's talked to your brother most recently. You'll want to get to know her and pick her brain."

I nodded.

She reached over and patted my shoulder. "You're not alone. You have a whole town behind you."

I nodded again. What in the hell else could I do? A whole town? Was she crazy?

She slipped out of my truck and walked around the front, then came around to my window. I rolled it down.

"I mean it, Kai. Ask for anything. We'll be here for you."

My throat was tight. All I could do was nod. She smiled and headed into her house.

Why hadn't I talked to Lettie sooner? I'd just been walking Chaos around the neighborhood and exploring downtown for the last couple of weeks and I hadn't even considered taking her to the woods.

Right now, my pup was in doggie heaven.

I looked in the rearview mirror.

"Aren't you, girl? You're loving life."

She couldn't hear me. She had her head out the window of the backseat of my Toyota 4Runner. I wished I had my head out the window. It was hot. And I mean *hot*. Lettie promised me that the forest trails up near the Whispering Pines Inn would be ten to fifteen degrees cooler, and I was counting on her being right. The last four days of one hundred-plus degree heat had me wilting. Yeah, there was air conditioning in the house. Beau hadn't skimped on any upgrade, but I just preferred the fresh air. I was a freak like that.

Of course, right now I had the air conditioning blowing in my car. I'd take advantage of it while I could. I'd be hot enough when I started my run. I took a turn and I'll be damned. Lettie was right, I was heading for a forest.

Duh, Marlowe. Hello, Smokey Mountains. Forests. Remember?

But still, I'd somehow thought they were farther away.

Now I was getting excited. If the trails were any good, today was going to be fantastic. I'd missed running.

I saw the sign for the Whispering Pines Inn, and I turned in. *What a cute building.* I loved the use of wood and glass for the façade; it looked both modern and foresty.

I laughed at my made-up word. Even so, it totally looked like it fit for the area. I was bummed that the trees weren't bumped up against it, but I knew that there needed to be a buffer zone between the forest and the dwelling in case of wildfires. Still, it would have looked pretty.

I pulled into the guest parking spot and got out of my 4Runner. As I started toward the front of the building, I could hear Chaos whining. I went back to my 4Runner.

I was such a pushover. Seriously, I needed to grow a backbone.

I popped the lock and gave my baby a long rub. "I'll be right back, then we'll go for a run. I promise." I pointed to my shorts and top. "Look, I'm dressed for running. Now no more whining, okay?"

She lay down on the back seat. "Good girl."

I heard a chuckle behind me. It wasn't the first time that somebody laughed at me talking to my girl. But it was the first time that a chuckle raced down my spine, swirled around until I felt it in my gut. I closed the backseat door and slowly turned around.

My eyes took in a tight white t-shirt that showed off a ripped abdomen and shoulders that I'd only seen in movies. Male legs encased in black bicycle shorts showed off thick, muscular thighs.

He chuckled again, and I realized I was staring.

Oh God. I'd never objectified a man like I had just now. I felt the heat climbing up my cheeks.

I looked up at his face and saw that he had a twinkle in his eye, and he was coming toward me.

His eyes.

His face.

"Beau? What are you doing here? I thought you were in Europe?"

He stopped in his tracks.

"Beau's in Europe?"

"What are you talking about?" I shook my head. "I talked to you six weeks ago. You said you would never be coming back here. Why are you here?"

"You talked to Beau?"

I shook my head again.

"Beau, what are you talking about?"

He walked closer, and was soon a foot away from me. He'd looked good ten yards away, but three feet away from me, he was overwhelming.

"Beau's my brother," he said softly.

"Your brother?" My voice was just as quiet as his had been. "Why didn't Beau tell me that he had a brother living here?"

He tilted his head and bit his lip and I thought I might melt into a puddle, and not because of the heat.

"Beau didn't know I'd be here. Are you the woman renting Beau's house?"

I nodded. It took more than a moment for me to find words. "What's your name?"

"Kai Davies."

"Hi." I took a deep breath. Enough of the breathy shit. "I'm Marlowe Jones." I thrust out my hand.

He took my hand, and I felt electricity spark. Honest-to-God electricity, like I had touched a live wire. I looked into his eyes and he looked as surprised as I was.

"Hello, Marlowe."

He let go of my hand and I sighed. I would have been fine having him hold my hand all day.

"Why wouldn't Beau have known you were here?"

"I grew up in Alaska. We didn't know about each other."

I tilted my head and frowned.

"It's complicated."

"Oh. I didn't mean to pry. Really, I didn't."

This left side of his mouth kicked up a bit, the same as his brother's. I remembered that was the best smile I ever got out of Beau, too. And I had worked hard to get him to smile.

"I didn't think you were prying, Marlowe. But it would have been fine if you were. I've learned that in this town, butting into everyone else's business is kind of the norm."

I giggled. Shit, when was the last time I actually giggled?

"You're right about that. I've only been living here for three weeks, and I swear that half the town knows my name and has read my resume."

He frowned. "Read your resume?"

"I applied to be the new high school math teacher. The school board had to vote. Apparently, the vote was during a public meeting and they read my resume out loud. The way Lettie tells it, there were a lot of opinions."

I watched as Beau's brother almost smiled.

"There were? What was the consensus?"

"Well, I got the job, but a lot of people wanted to see a picture of me. They were worried that a pretty, single female might be too distracting for their boys."

"They must not have had a picture handy, since you're not pretty, you're beautiful."

I rolled my eyes. "Geesh, let's not go overboard. And anyway, none of the boys in my classes ever found me to be a distraction in the past."

"Sure, they haven't," he teased. "Instead, they've all been lining up for extra credit and extra tutoring."

Damn. He was right. "Umm, I think I need to go in and check-in with Gretchen. Lettie told me that there were some great running trails around here that I could take my dog on."

This time Beau actually did smile, and what a smile it was. He had laugh lines that fanned out at his eyes, and his teeth gleamed white like he was some kind of model.

"Enjoy your run."

"What about you? It looks like you're suited up for a run."

"Cycling. My running days are over. These days I road ride, less impact. My bike's over there." He pointed to a bright green gravel bike leaning up against the stairs.

"Injury?"

He nodded.

"Damn, that's a tough break. I'm sorry, but at least you can ride."

"That's how I see it."

"Enjoy your day."

He didn't move, instead he continued to stare at me.

Please ask me out. Please ask me out.

"I don't suppose you'd like to grab lunch sometime?"

I stopped myself from doing a fist pump.

"I would absolutely love to grab lunch sometime." I grinned.

"I don't have my phone with me."

I turned around and opened the driver's side door and fished my phone out of my purse. "Give me your number, and I'll call it, then you'll have mine." He gave me his number and I dialed it.

"You free tomorrow?" he asked.

Oh boy was I.

"Yep," I said calmly.

"Okay, then I can pick you up at your house at eleven-thirty, how does that sound?"

"You know where I live?"

"You're renting Beau's house, right?"

I frowned. "How do you know that?"

"Lettie told me."

I shook my head and smiled. "It sure is a small town. Yeah, pick me up tomorrow."

He held out his hand and I juggled my phone so I

could shake his. It was the same as before, but this time I was ready for it. The jolt of electricity shot through my hand, up my arm, and I savored it.

What would happen if we kissed?

7

Dress or jeans?

Dress or jeans?

Dress or jeans?

I looked at the pile of clothes on my bed and winced. Really? I was acting worse than one of my old high school students.

I jumped when I heard my phone ring.

"Thank God!"

I started rifling through all the clothes on my bed, trying to find my cell phone. "Please let it be Sue."

When I found it, I immediately answered it. "Where have you been?!"

"Stop the suit," a weird voice said.

"Huh?"

"Stop the lawsuit."

"What? Who is this?"

"If you don't stop the suit, you'll be sorry."

"Who are you?"

I realized I was talking to a dial tone. Come to think of it, the weird voice sounded like some kind of voice modification device, which only made the whole thing creepier. I looked down at my phone and hit the 'recent' button. The call came from an unknown number.

Shit, I'd always known that the unlawful termination suit I had filed against Principal Sykes would be an uphill climb, but this was ridiculous.

"Ughhhh!"

I dropped my phone when it rang again.

"Quit being a baby," I muttered as I picked up the phone and then saw it was Sue. I noted the time. I only had twenty more minutes to get dressed for my date. Thank God my hair was done. Make-up consisted of mascara and lip gloss. So now it was just shoes and clothes.

"Sue! I need your help. Dress or jeans?" I wailed.

"Are you trying to tell me that my friend who swore off men after Denny, is actually going on a date?"

"We agreed never to mention that man's name again."

"I never agreed to that. He was lower than a slug. He had you believing that it was because of you it was okay for him to cheat. That asshole was gaslighting you so bad it took a year for you to get away from him."

"But I did. And that was four years ago and two years of counseling, so yes. I'm going on a date."

"Tell me about him."

"I hardly know anything about him. We're going out for lunch. His brother owns the house I'm renting—"

"The hottie brother, Beau? The guy who's in the military?"

"Yeah, that's the one."

"Does he look like him?"

"Almost identical. Except I saw Kai smile. It wasn't like a big smile or anything, but it was a smile. They both have the scruff thing going on that comes out red and gold, but his hair is that luscious auburn color that every woman in the world would kill for."

"So he's not a carrot-top?"

"Nope," I confirmed.

"And eyes?"

"Light blue. But when he laughs, they flash silver. Now answer my question—jeans or a dress?"

"Where are you going to lunch?"

"There are really only two places to go to lunch in this town, both of them diners. People will be dressed any old way."

"What's the weather like?"

"Hot." I eyed my yellow sundress. It had a daisy pattern along the bottom of the skirt, with two small white lace straps going over each shoulder. It was really feminine. I'd only ever worn it once. I'd bought it shopping with Sue on a lark.

"If it's hot, wear a dress and sandals. Do you have any sundresses?" she asked.

"Yes. I have three to choose from, but remember the one we bought at Belk?"

"The Daisy Duke?"

"Stop calling it that," I demanded. "It is not slutty. It's cute and only shows a little ta-ta."

Sue laughed. "Honey, with you, there's no such thing as a little ta-ta."

I growled and Sue laughed some more.

"The dress is perfect. Especially if you like the guy. Do you like him?"

"It's too early to tell. But I *could* like him."

"Then go out with guns blazing. It's best to hook 'em and throw 'em back, then realize you like 'em and realize you didn't hook 'em."

"What's with all the fish talk?" I asked.

"I went fishing with my dad last weekend."

"You're such a good daughter. I love your dad."

"He asked about you, Marlowe. He wanted to know when that bullshit lawsuit was going to be over and you could come back to work here in West Virginia."

"Did you explain to him that even if I win, I'm not going to work at that school again?" I picked up the dress off my bed and pulled it over my head. Thank God it had a side zipper.

"I tried to tell him that. Then he wanted to know what the point was."

"Did he get it? Did he understand I didn't want that bad mark on my resume anymore?"

"Yeah, that, he understood."

Chaos nosed her way into my bedroom and sat down to give me the onceover. I went to the dresser and pulled on some bangles and a couple of rings, then I pushed in some big hoop silver earrings. I fluffed my hair, then went to the bathroom and bent over. Chaos was still following me, but when she saw me pick up the can of hairspray, she ran out of the bathroom so fast, I heard her skid on the hardware floor of the bedroom. Laughing, I sprayed my hair.

"Can you hear me?" Sue shouted.

"Now I can. I was putting on hairspray."

"Are you in the daisy dress?"

"Yep."

"What shoes?"

"Red wedges with the ankle straps."

"Nice. Call me when you get home."

"Yes, Mom." I laughed. So did Sue. Then she hung up.

Chaos came into my bedroom again, sniffing the air.

"It's all clear," I assured her.

She let out a low *woof*.

"Are you going to be a good girl while I'm gone?"

Woof.

"You have your doggy door that Beau let me have built. So, you're good to go. Literally," I grinned. I picked up my phone off the bed and remembered the threatening phone call. It was the third one I'd received. It was time for me to let my attorney know about it, but I hated to sound like a wuss. Maybe I could just wait a little bit more. After all, they were just phone calls.

Woof.

Woof.

Woof.

Chaos always alerted me before the knock on the door or the bell would ring. I wondered how she would take Kai. She was a good judge of character. As a matter of fact, I wished that I had had her before I'd met Denny. The couple of times we'd run into him in Danville, after I had got her, she'd tried really hard to get at him. She hadn't liked him at all.

"Be a good girl," I whispered as I stroked her neck. Then I whispered in her ear. "But not too good. Let me know if he's a good guy or not."

I opened the door and all the breath left my body. Kai was clean-shaven and his curls were under control. He was smiling. I worried that my mouth was hanging open at the beauty of Kai.

"Hi, Marlowe. Are you going to introduce me?"

I looked down and saw Chaos playing peek-a-boo behind my skirt.

Really?

"Shy?" Kai asked.

"Not normally." I shook my head. "This is a first."

Kai squatted down and I got to watch his powerful thighs flex in his jeans.

I needed ice water. *Fast.*

"Boy or a girl?" he asked as he held out his hand for Chaos to sniff.

"A girl who I swear is flirting. I have never seen her behave like this in my life."

"How long have you had her?" he asked as he looked up at me.

I had trouble thinking of an answer as those blue-silver eyes focused on me. I stared down at him.

"Marlowe?"

"Uhm. I've had her since she was weaned."

Chaos came out from behind me, wagging her tail. Kai started to scratch my girl under her chin, and the little slut was groaning in delight. What was even worse is, I was envious.

After long moments, Kai stood up.

"Well, we better go. We don't want to miss out on the apple pie."

"Pearl's or Down Home?" I asked.

"I usually do Pearl's for dinner. I enjoy seeing Little Grandma, so I'll do breakfast or lunch at the Down Home Diner." He went to open the door for me, then he paused. "Your girl took me by surprise and I didn't have a chance to tell you just how beautiful you look in your dress."

I had to be as red as a lobster who'd just been dunked in boiling water. I tried to will away the blush, but I knew it wasn't working. At least it was summer, and I'd been getting a little bit of a tan, so maybe it wasn't quite as obvious, right?

I peeked up at Kai and saw him grinning down at me. Nope, no luck. He'd cottoned onto my blush.

"Umm, thank you." I muttered.

"Are you going to be able to handle it if I also tell you I really enjoy seeing your hair down? I can't wait to see what it'll look like in the sun."

I shuddered, and he laughed.

"Okay, come on, let's go. I promise not to tell you what I think about your shoes."

I hadn't been teasing about how beautiful she looked in the dress. The side benefit of complimenting her on her hair and shoes, was seeing her blush. It was like no man had ever given her a compliment before.

I refrained from telling her how good her ass looked, but it had been a thing of beauty as she had climbed into my truck before I had shut her in.

For the last four days I tried to make sense of why I had asked her out. This wasn't part of the plan. I wanted to know more about my mother and brother, and dating someone who was new to town wasn't going to help me down that path.

She is living in your old house.

So?

If you look inside you might remember more things.

Now you're reaching.

"Are you okay?"

"Huh?"

"I asked you a couple of times how you knew Lettie."

I frowned. Dammit, I really had been off in la-la land.

"I met her at the Down Home Diner. She drove me past your house, because she knew that's where Beau grew up. She's Little Grandma's daughter, right?"

Marlowe laughed. "She's her granddaughter. Patty is Little Grandma's daughter. She cooks at the diner, and she's Lettie's mom."

I shook my head. "There's a lot to keep straight."

"That part is simple. Wait until you get to Patty's sisters and their kids and grandkids. That's when it really gets interesting."

"I thought you said you'd only been here for a few weeks."

"I went over to Lettie's for a potluck. I got to meet a lot of the family."

"Who else have you met?"

I glanced over at her and saw her concentrating.

"I have to tell you; I was a little overwhelmed at the potluck. There had to be fifty to sixty people coming in and out of her house and in her backyard. I did meet another big family."

"Who were they?"

"Originally, they were all known as the Averys. One brother and six sisters who'd been born and raised here, but now some girls are married, so their last names aren't Avery anymore."

"How many did you meet?"

"I didn't meet their brother. He's in the Navy and stationed in San Diego." She paused. "No, that's not right. He lives there. He's stationed in Corona."

"Coronado?"

"Yeah, that's it. Evie, that's one of the Avery girls, told me that. Her husband is stationed there too. Her name is Evie O'Malley now. Both her husband and her brother work together."

They had to be SEALs.

"Who else did you meet?"

"I met the oldest Avery sister. Her name is Trenda Clark. Her husband was there. His name is Simon Clark, but her daughter Bella, took the cake. She is a pistol. She's nine or ten years old, and she knew everything about everyone. Simon is her stepdaddy, but she loves him to death, and calls him daddy. Apparently, he was a SEAL Commander, but since he settled down here in Jasper Creek, he started up a security company. I would bet my bottom dollar Simon's head would explode if he knew how much private information she gave out."

"I bet you're right."

"But it wasn't just about her daddy. She told me about how she was kidnapped by a bad man with Millie and Lisa."

Luckily, I was pulling up to a stop sign when she shared that bit of information. "Kidnapped?"

"She then went on to say it was okay because her daddy saved her."

"What?"

"Seriously, that's what she said. When I asked her how, that was when Trenda stepped in. She said to quit trying to scare away the new residents." She giggled. "Bella waited until her mother left, then told me, that I didn't have to worry about anything because her daddy and Roan could beat up anybody and keep me safe."

"Do you think what the kid was saying was true?"

"I ended up sitting at a table with Roan and Lisa, and I mentioned what Bella had said. Lisa told me she'd had a stalker that had followed her from her old town. She tried to shrug it off, but Roan looked pissed. Not that Bella had said something, more that Lisa had been in danger."

I could totally understand that. If someone I cared about was in danger, I'd be pissed. Pissed and scared. Mainly pissed until I took that asshole down.

I pulled up to a good parking spot near the Down Home Diner. Someone must have just left. I really liked the town center. There wasn't a speck of trash to be seen, and on every streetlight hung a basket of flowers.

Marlowe started to open the passenger door.

"Wait for me to get it."

After having been stationed in North Carolina, you pick up a few things. One was Southern gentleman manners. I sure as hell didn't learn them from my father.

I went around the front of the truck and opened

her door. I held out my hand to help her out. I enjoyed seeing the length of leg that was on display as she stepped onto the running board and then down to the street.

"I've been here for breakfast, but I haven't been here for lunch," Marlowe admitted.

"Then you're in for a treat."

8

"Brady, I have a table near the window waiting for you."

"Little Grandma, how'd you know I was coming in for lunch?"

"Just a feeling I had."

I shivered. I hated feelings like that. They reminded me too much of my dreams, too much of that woman Blessing. But I forced myself to smile.

"And who are you?" The old woman smiled at Marlowe.

"I'm sorry. I forgot my manners. This is Marlowe Jones. She's renting Beau's place."

Little Grandma smiled. "You're the new math teacher. Aren't you pretty as a picture?" She turned on her stool. I knew she was getting ready to holler for Lettie, but her granddaughter was already beside her, grinning.

"Hey, you two. Your table is waiting. Follow me."

Lettie seated them in the far corner, like we needed privacy. I appreciated it.

"What can I get you two to drink?"

"Iced tea for me," Marlowe answered.

"I'll take water."

Lettie plopped down the menus and left us, and Marlowe laughed. "We're going to be the talk of the town."

"Huh?"

"The two of us eating here, both of us not wearing jeans? It's looking date-like. Yep, this will be all over Jasper Creek by tomorrow morning."

"I think you've got this wrong. People have better things to do with their lives than gossip."

Marlowe laughed again, and I couldn't help but be affected. It was low and husky and it hit me in my gut.

"You were in the service, right?"

I nodded.

"How long?"

"Fourteen years."

She tilted her head and grinned. "Are you telling me that there wasn't scuttlebutt flying around base when people hooked up?"

"Scuttlebutt? What are you doing using a Navy term?"

"My dad was in the Navy," Marlowe said quietly. "I lost him, my mom, and my sister in a car wreck when I was in college."

"Aw, Marlowe, I'm so sorry." I looked into her

eyes, and could see how her brown eyes were almost black. There was a shine to them, as if she were getting ready to cry. Then she took a deep breath, and as if by magic, her eyes were their normal warm brown, and no sign of tears.

"Yeah, it was rough, but I've mostly moved past it." She gave me a smile.

I shook my head. "You never get over something like that. It haunts you, and then something will trigger you and it will come up and hit you in the heart."

"Have you lost someone?" I saw an imperceptible tremble of her lower lip, but then she pushed them tightly together.

I thought about Sully, and I nodded. "It was nothing compared to you. But one of our teammates suffered a stroke while we were on leave. We were in Hawaii for a couple of days before heading to Japan to go skiing on Mt. Fuji. Sully had a massive stroke and he never woke up."

Marlowe bent her head, then looked up. "That's rough."

I nodded. She must have noticed my fist clenched on the table, because she put her hand over mine. It felt strange having someone trying to comfort me. Strange and good. But how could it be possible when what happened to her was ten times worse? I turned my hand over and tangled my fingers with hers. She let me. This felt even better.

"Here's your iced tea, Honey." Lettie placed our

brimming glasses down on the table without spilling a drop and Marlowe took that moment to pull back her hand.

I wanted her hand back. I wanted her touch.

I was beginning to like this woman.

"So have you decided what you want to order?"

"Do you have fried chicken?" Marlowe asked.

Lettie grinned. "Haven't had time to look at the menu, have you? Your best bet is to go with the buttermilk brined fried chicken with our spicy maple syrup, served up with the fluffiest waffles you can imagine."

"She's not lying," a man's voice shouted out.

I looked over to see Harvey sitting two tables over.

"After watching you eat at Lettie's potluck, I know you know your food. So, I trust you, Harvey." Marlowe grinned.

"Actually, you can't trust him. If I served him pig slop, he'd eat it, as long as I covered it up with enough gravy."

"You wound me, Lettie. I might have to take my business elsewhere," Harvey complained.

"Don't lie to me, Harvey Sadowski. Pearl cut you off for two days, seeing as how you told her the eggs were too runny and the bacon was burnt."

Marlowe and I were doing our best not to laugh. She was having better luck. Harvey was reminding me of one of my old Sergeants, and I was about to lose it.

"Lettie, what could I do? Sam's been off his game, I had to bring it to Pearl's attention. She didn't want her customers to be upset."

"You yelled it across the restaurant so everybody could hear. Including Sam. He's going through a lot, and there you were poking at him. It wasn't just rude, it was mean."

Lettie's voice had lowered at the last sentence. Apparently, what she had to say was relatively private. I took in Harvey's face. He was beginning to look upset. He got out of his chair and stood next to our table so he could talk to Lettie privately.

"Lettie, what's wrong with Sam? Now that you've said this much, you've got to tell me the rest. You know it will go no further than me and Missy."

"That's what I'm afraid of. I know Missy and she'll be over at his house offering him meals and her help an hour after you hang up the phone with her. You and I know Sam won't want that."

This entire conversation was fascinating. Missy had to be Harvey's wife, and she knew who Sam was and where he lived. Sam had to be sick and she would be going over to his house to help him, just based on one conversation. This place really was something special.

"Lettie, cut it out and just tell me. I'll make sure that Missy stays put until you, Pearl or Little Grandma gives me the go-ahead. How 'bout that?"

Lettie sighed, then nodded. "Sam had a stroke four weeks ago. That's why he wasn't in the kitchen

CAITLYN O'LEARY

for a couple of weeks. He insisted on coming back, but he's struggling. Pearl wanted him to only come back part time, but he wouldn't hear of it."

"Pearl's scary," Harvey muttered. "All she needed to do was put her foot down."

"She's set up like we are," Lettie said. "We have insurance for the few full-time folks we have, but our sick leave and vacation is minimal. Pearl was paying over and above for Sam. Hell, he'd been working for Pearl since damn near day one. That's why he insisted on coming back. He knew she was paying him out of her own pocket, while paying someone to come in and cook."

"Damn, Lettie, why didn't she tell us? You know we would have been over like a shot. The man doesn't have any family."

"You know Sam's too proud for that. But Pearl told me and Ma and Little Grandma, so we went over in shifts when Pearl had to stay at her restaurant. It was easier for us, since we close the diner at four."

Harvey nodded. "How bad was the stroke, Lettie?"

"It wasn't good, but you know how it is these days. They boot you out of the hospital as soon as you can blink on your own." Lettie sighed. "Okay, it wasn't as bad as that, but Sam lied to them and said he had someone at home who would be there to take care of him. His left side isn't good, he's having trouble with his left leg still, his left shoulder and arm are getting somewhat better. Pearl gives him and her other two full-time employees insurance, but it's not

98

the best, so rehab was out of the question, so I got him exercises off the internet to do."

I winced. The longer Sam went without doing proper physical therapy, the more likely he was to not recover his full range of motion. What's more, his pain could get really bad if his muscles atrophy and joints contracture.

Fuck!

Kai, you're not here to get involved. You just wanted to find out where you came from and maybe meet your brother. You didn't want to get involved. Remember?

"Is there a physical therapist in town who could work with him?" I asked.

Harvey and Lettie's gazes swung to me. It was obvious they had forgotten that Marlowe and I were sitting at the table.

"No, no physical therapist," Harvey answered. "There's only Doc Evans who's about Little Grandma's age. For anything more than a sliver removed, you need to go to Gatlinburg."

"Shame on you." Lettie glowered at Harvey. "He's my mom's age, and he's delivered most everybody here in Jasper Creek."

"Which explains why most of the population of Jasper Creek is a few bricks shy of a load."

"Starting with you, Harvey Sandowski. Starting with you," Lettie muttered, shaking her head.

"Nah, I was delivered when he was still at the top of his game," Harvey chortled.

"Apparently you weren't, if you're dumb enough

to be talking about me when I'm three tables away from you."

Am I in a fucking soap opera or what?

I watched as a gray-haired old man walked over to our table. Despite the gray hair, he seemed pretty spry. Actually, he was moving a whole hell of a lot better than Harvey was. I bet he wasn't eating the cardiac kicker for every meal.

"Lettie, I have to say I'm very disappointed in you, your ma, your grandma, and Pearl for not telling me about Sam. I could have helped some."

"You were taking care of Carrie and her son. You didn't need anything more put on your plate," Lettie protested.

Doc Evans ran his hand through what was left of his white hair and sighed. "Carrie and Rick were out of the woods last week, and you know it. You could have brought me in then."

"By that time, Sam was back at work," Lettie disagreed. "There wasn't anything you could do."

"I could have helped with his exercises."

"You needed some downtime. Anyway, the last time someone needed PT, you sent them to Gatlinburg, and Sam doesn't have the money for that."

I cleared my throat, and all three of them looked down at me. "I could help with the PT."

"Are you a physical therapist?" the doctor asked.

"No, but I spent six months at Walter Reed getting physical therapy on my back, arm, and leg. I know how important it is, and I know how to do the exercises properly. I can talk to my physical therapist and ask him which exercises Sam needs, and then help him do them properly."

I watched as Doc Evans again ran his hand through his sparce hair. No wonder he was almost bald. "So, you're the missing Brady Beaumont, huh? How long are you planning on sticking around for?"

I shouldn't have been surprised that he knew who I was. Apparently, everybody knew everything about one another in this town.

"I go by Kai." I stood up and offered my hand. "Kai Davies."

"I didn't deliver you and your brother. I was worried about delivering twins, so you were delivered in Gatlinburg."

I nodded. That filled in some blanks.

"So, your son-of-a-bitch father took you?"

I nodded.

"He hurt you?" The doctor gave me a piercing look.

"Nothing I couldn't handle."

I heard Marlowe gasp. "The bastard hurt you." The doctor made it a statement. A statement I couldn't dispute. "He was worse than a son-of-a-bitch. He was evil. Left town before he could be arrested after what he did to your brother. I assume because you're calling yourself Kai Davies that you didn't know about that."

I shook my head. "Only reason I'm here is that I found a photo of Beau and me when we were maybe three years old in the front yard of our house. The one with the red porch swing. On the back of the photo, it said Brady and Grady, Jasper Creek."

"If he was calling you Kai Davies, what was he calling himself?"

"Ronald Davies," I answered.

"Hmmm. I expect the statute of limitations is done for kidnapping you, then again, maybe not." Again, he rubbed the top of his head. "We'll have to call Nash."

Now I wanted to scrub the top of my head. The last thing I wanted to do was file charges against Ronald/Arthur. I wanted him in my rearview mirror, and I wanted to stay here long enough to meet my brother, which might take more than a minute.

"Eh-hum, you both have forgotten what's important. Sam is who we were talking about." Lettie looked over at me. "When can you start working with Sam? He gets off at seven o'clock."

"I'm thinking since I'm a stranger, somebody better talk to him about me first, don't ya think?" I worked hard to keep the sarcasm out of my voice, but from the way Lettie rolled her eyes and Doc laughed, apparently I didn't succeed.

"He's got you there, Lettie," the Doc laughed.

"All right. Leave your number at the checkout stand when you leave. I'll call you tomorrow on how to get to Sam's house."

I just nodded. She was a steamroller, and I knew I

was hired. Not that I was going to get any money, and not that I cared. Uncle Sam was giving me disability pay, and I'd never been a big spender so I had a nice nest egg that I still needed to figure out what to do with.

"Now the rest of you lot, get to your seats, your food is getting cold."

"So, does that mean Missy and I can take some food over to Sam's?"

Lettie slammed her fists on her hips and looked up at Harvey. "No. Weren't you listening, you big lug? He needs to be feeling better about himself before he can take anybody knowing that anything went wrong. Let Kai here do his magic. Get back to your seat."

I watched as Harvey and Doc went back to their seats then turned my attention to Lettie.

"I'm not sure what I'm actually going to be able to do," I objected.

Lettie glanced over at me. "I know your type. Always hiding your light under a bushel. If you said you know something about physical therapy, that means you could probably hang out a shingle."

Marlowe laughed.

"See, even Marlowe agrees with me, and it's only your first date."

"How do you know everything?"

"It's the way it is around here. Get used to it." She turned to Marlowe and smiled. "So, do you want the fried chicken and waffles?"

Marlowe had the widest smile on her face that I'd ever seen. Man, she was pretty.

"Lettie, you sold me. I'd love that."

"What about you, Kai?"

"Surprise me."

Lettie and Marlowe both chuckled.

"I like it. A man of adventure," Marlowe crooned.

The tone of her voice streaked straight to my cock. Then she put her straw in her iced tea and took a delicate sip, and I knew I was in big trouble.

9

He was giving me a strange look. His gaze was so intense, it made my heart race. Why was he looking at me like that? I tilted my head, seeing if he would tell me what he was thinking, but he didn't. Instead, he shook his head.

"Sounds like I really stepped in it," he finally said.

"When you say it that way, it makes it sound like you stepped in something by accident. You were totally aware of what you were signing up for."

His smile was rueful. "You're right. I did."

"Why did you?"

"I've been where Sam is."

"You mentioned Walter Reed. Now I'll admit that Lettie already said you were in the military. But she hadn't said you'd been badly injured."

"Only Little Grandma knows about my injury. Well, and you," Kai said.

"I'm not surprised she didn't mention it. She

seems like the type of lady who keeps her own counsel."

Kai nodded in agreement.

"I wonder just how much she knows about this town?" I pondered.

"I would guess, everything."

I laughed. "I'm thinking you're right about that." I paused, feeling the weight of the next question.

"Go ahead and ask. I already liked how up front you were up in the woods the other day. You just said it was a tough break, and we moved on. Don't start pussyfooting around things now."

"I gotcha. So how long were you in Walter Reed?"

"I got injured overseas. To begin with I was airlifted to the American military hospital in Germany. That's where they did the original surgeries. They weren't sure that I was going to make it."

I sucked in a deep breath. "What was wrong?"

"Two sniper bullets hit close to me. The shards from the concrete that blew off the building hit me. I had my Kevlar on, but it hit me along the back of my neck, or what the docs call the cervical spine. I don't remember much of anything after that happened."

"How long were you in Germany?"

"Two months. They don't usually keep you that long at Landstuhl, but I ended up with an infection. When they sent me to the US, they told me that I wasn't going to walk again. I stayed at Walter Reed for eight months. Six months was in rehab."

The grin on his face was really something to

behold. It made my stomach flip in a way I wasn't prepared for. He was telling me something serious, and here I was, feeling like a teenager.

"So you enjoyed your physical therapy?" I asked, trying to get myself back on track.

"I enjoyed the *results* of the PT, that's for damn sure. But to give you an idea of how much I liked the physical therapy, to this day I refer to my physical therapist as the demon from hell. But by God, he got me to the point that I can jog and bicycle. So I'm damn happy."

"That's amazing, Kai." I couldn't imagine being in his shoes. I admired his strength, his determination. "What did you do in the service? Do you think that helped you push yourself to walk?"

"Here's your food," Lettie said. She put a big plate in front of me that smelled heavenly, but it was piled to the moon.

"Lettie, I'm not going to be able to eat all of this," I protested.

I watched as she put another big plate in front of Kai, only it was filled with broccoli, cauliflower, corn, and turkey.

"Don't worry about it, Marlowe. I expect that Kai will be eating whatever you can't finish."

I looked over at Kai. He winked at me. "I've got your back."

I nearly melted right then.

"See, I told you." Lettie patted my shoulder. "Is there anything else I can get for you?"

We both shook our heads, and then started eating. After my second bite of fried chicken and my first bite of waffle, I looked up at Kai. "You're not going to be getting *any* of my food."

He burst out laughing. The sound was deep, rich, and sent tingles down my spine. "In that case, I'll put in another order to take back to the hotel with me."

"How long are you staying at Whispering Pines?"

"Until I get in touch with Beau."

"Are you going to talk to Bernie? He's the one who arranged the three calls I had with Beau."

"Yeah, he's definitely on my list of people to talk to." Kai cut up a piece of turkey and put it in his mouth. When he was done chewing and swallowing, he gave me a half smile. "You were also on my list of people to talk to, even if I didn't want to ask you out."

"So, is this a date?" I teased.

He leaned in slightly, lowering his voice, making it impossible for me to look anywhere but at him— not that I wanted to. "If you don't know this is a date, I'm doing something wrong. How can I convince you?"

I shivered. "I think you telling me I was beautiful and noticing my shoes, convinced me."

"Don't forget your hair. Now that I've seen it down, I'm going to be dreaming about your hair."

Damn, I'm going to start blushing again.

Time for a new topic. "What do you want to know about Beau?"

"Anything? Everything?" He took a sip of water.

"Now I probably sound like one of those lovelorn high school boys who follow you around."

"No. No, you don't. You sound exactly like a brother who wants to know about a twin he never knew he had."

"That's not quite true. I had dreams of the two of us. I remember telling my father about them once…"

His voice trailed off.

"And?" I prompted.

"Let's just say, it didn't go well, and leave it at that."

I could see both pain and anger in his eyes. My instinct was to reach out, touch his hand, offer some comfort. I sure as hell wasn't going to press for an answer. "Was there anything good about your childhood?" I prayed he'd say yes.

His expression softened. The anger left his eyes. "Alaska is beautiful. Before I turned ten, I got to run wild. Dillingham is a small community, and I made friends with other kids who were just as unruly as I was. Ronald, I mean Arthur, didn't care where I was, or who I was with. It was great. Then I turned ten and I had to work the boat."

"I don't understand. What do you mean, work the boat?"

"He owned a crabbing boat. He was a shitty captain, but he somehow managed to talk some guys into working the boat with him during king crab season from October to January. He had less guys working for him during snow and Dungeness season because they weren't worth as much, so the payout was smaller. That's why he needed me. Plus, I was cheap labor."

"Was it dangerous?"

Kai gave me a half grin.

"Sometimes."

The way he said sometimes didn't sound like he was shutting me out like the way he had earlier. So, I decided to ask more questions. "What did you have to do on a crab ship?"

"A crab ship?" He grinned. "You're cute. It's a crabber. We would bait two hundred crab pots and throw them over the side."

"How would you keep track of so many?"

"We would attach a buoy to each one and drop it over the side. I was lucky. Sometimes I didn't have to bait the traps and help throw them over the side. Instead, Ronald would have me record the location, depth, date, and time each pot was set."

"Weren't those heavy?"

"Not as heavy as the full pots."

"How heavy were those?"

"Anywhere from five- to eight-hundred pounds."

I'd been in the middle of pouring the spicy maple syrup onto my meal, and I dropped it. "You had to help pull those into the crabber? And you were ten? And some of them were eight-hundred pounds?"

He nodded.

"When you were ten?" I repeated, trying to wrap my head around it.

"Marlowe, it's no big deal. What's more, the crew decided I was more of a hindrance at ten, so they had me help sort out the small crabs and females that needed to be thrown back. When I was twelve, Ronald noticed this and raised holy hell, so I had to start pulling in the traps like the rest of the crew."

"My God, Kai. Was there anything good after you had to start crabbing?"

He frowned. I could see him thinking, then he gave me a slow smile.

"I remember this one time, we were crabbing in Bristol Bay. We'd dumped off our catch at Dutch Harbor. I was fourteen. It was the biggest haul we'd ever made. Ronald went to King Salmon instead of Dillingham. I didn't see Ronald for an entire week. The guys said there was some woman he went to see. I didn't care, as long as I didn't have to be with him."

"He just left you alone?" My heart went out to the fourteen-year-old boy he'd been.

"Yep." Kai grinned. "Like I said, this was a good time. I didn't get paid. But I did have a place to sleep. Of course, it was in the shittiest motel that Ronald could find. It made the LeeHy motel look like the Waldorf. But Lucky, Barry, and Shil decided it would be a good time to show me more of Alaska. They used some of their money to fly us all to Sitka. Have you ever been to Alaska?" Kai asked me.

I shook my head.

"Have you seen pictures?"

"Sure."

"They wanted to show me the fjords. This was about twenty years ago, before it started warming. They were mind blowing, Marlowe. Just stunning. You would see this white snow, covering crevices of neon blue. But it wasn't just the visuals, you could taste them. The cold air was an icy blast that coated your lungs with a fresh taste that made you feel like you took in a breath of heaven."

I stared at him. He was looking off in the distance. I'd wanted to kiss him before he'd said that, but now, I *really* wanted to kiss him. "That sounds beautiful. What else did you do?"

"Besides taking a boat ride to see the fjords, I fished."

"Fished? Hadn't you'd been on a boat long enough already?"

"No, we didn't go on a boat, we stood out in the middle of a river. They got me a special rod and reel and tried to teach me fly fishing. It wasn't until day three that I finally started getting the hang of it, but it was soothing to be out there with the guys, just standing out in the river with your wading boots on, feeling the river flow by and the rustle of the wind in the trees. It made you feel closer to nature. It was one of the best times of my life."

I sighed. "Hearing that makes me feel better. I'm glad you had friends like that in your life. I'm sorry I got you off track. Let me tell you about Beau."

Kai put his fork down, and I had his full attention.

"First, let me just tell you, I don't have a lot to tell

you. Yes, I had three conversations with him, but we talked in total for maybe a half hour."

"Still, that's a lot, considering the fact you were just talking about you renting his house."

"He was curious as to why I was coming to Jasper Creek to teach, so I told him my little story, so that took a bit."

"What happened?"

I didn't want to get into my story, didn't want to think about *my* life at the moment. "Uh-uh, we already got off track once. Back to Beau. To begin with I thought he was a flake. Bernie would set-up a FaceTime meeting and he wouldn't show. It wasn't until the third meeting that we met."

Kai started to frown but I shook my head before he could get upset. "No, don't get a bad opinion of him. He's active duty. The guy here in Jasper Creek who normally handles the renting of the house wasn't available."

Kai relaxed and sat back. "Good. I can't imagine him blowing you off on purpose." He gave me the kind of smile that made me lose track of what we were even talking about.

My plate was still mostly full, but I couldn't eat another bite. It might have had something to do with the way my heart kept fluttering. "You're in luck. You don't have to order chicken and waffles to go. There is no way I can finish this. Wanna trade plates?" It was something I saw Mom and Dad do all the time.

His eyes lit up. "Sure." He switched the plates and

I had an empty plate in front of me, and he had a mound of chicken and a good deal of waffles in front of him. "If you see Lettie, flag her down. I'm definitely going to need more syrup."

"Can your body handle sugar?" I teased. He was made of pure muscle.

"Only when I'm on a date, then my body demands sugar."

The way he was looking at me, there was no way I could miss his meaning.

Gah! I felt myself blushing again.

"Beau was actually a good guy once I had a chance to talk to him. He wanted to know about my dog."

"Chaos?"

"Yeah. I'd put her down on the application. A lot of the places I'd looked at here in Jasper Creek wouldn't rent to someone with a pet. Beau would, but he still wanted to know about her. I got the feeling it was more curiosity than worry."

"Why did you think that?"

I thought back to our conversation. "He had a lot of questions about her like her breed, her age, what kind of personality she had, how long I'd had her. Things like that. Did you guys have a dog?"

Kai squeezed the bridge of his nose and closed his eyes, and I regretted opening up another hidden wound. Then he looked at me. "Not that I can remember. But I remember as a kid always wanting one. Ronald wasn't having it. Two of the kids I hung out with had dogs, it was great playing with them.

Nobody enforced a leash law in Dillingham. We were constantly running wild with the dogs."

Talk about a man who needed a dog.

"So, what did Beau think when you told him you had a Bernese Mountain dog?"

My heart stuttered. He'd met Chaos, but only a real dog lover would know her breed. "How'd you know what kind of breed Chaos was?"

He shrugged. "Just picked it up, here and there."

I lifted my glass of tea. "Here's to the college of 'Here and There.'"

I grinned when he laughed. He had a great laugh.

"I enjoyed talking to your brother, but here's the moment I liked your brother. It was after I had moved in and we FaceTimed for the last time. I was bemoaning the fact that I was probably going to need to use my school lunchbreaks to come back home to let Chaos out. I told Beau how at my old house in West Virginia, the property was big enough and off the beaten track, that having a big doggy door wasn't a security issue."

"Let me guess. Beau came up with a way for you to have a doggy door in his house that Chaos could use."

"How'd you know?"

"Just a wild guess."

Talk about bullshit.

"Well Mr. Smartypants, he figured out a way that only Chaos could go in or out of the door, if we put a chip in her collar. He even told me who I should talk to, to have the door installed. And he insisted on paying half of the installation, because it was an upgrade for the house."

Kai hit me with another of those killer smiles that put me back in danger of melting into a puddle right there. "He did that part because you're beautiful."

My face felt like it turned to flames. "He's just a nice guy. There was no flirting going on."

Kai's eyebrow lifted and he looked amused. "Let me guess—he offered to pay for the total installation."

I nodded.

"There was flirting going on."

I blushed as I took a long sip of my iced tea.

Should I say it? Before I could talk myself out of it, I blurted, "Not like with you and me."

Kai stared at me so hard, it was as if he thought I was going to vanish.

He only looked away long enough to signal to Lettie for the check.

10

I couldn't get her out of the diner fast enough. Not after that comment. And not after watching her play with her straw. The way her lips wrapped around it and her fingers played. We went back to her house.

No. Not her house. Beau's house. The house that I'd lived a different life in, one I couldn't remember but that haunted my dreams.

"Do you want to come inside?" she asked me, that same look in her eyes she'd given me at the diner.

I stood on the porch with the red swing, and I was sweating. I wish I could say it was because of the heat and the look in her eyes, but I knew better. It was being here. This place. If I went inside, it would make it all real. That this had once been my home. That Mom and Grady were real. That I'd lost them, all because of Ronald.

It was getting even hotter. Ants were crawling under every inch of my skin.

Stinging.

Biting.

I jumped.

"God I'm sorry." Marlowe jerked her hand away from my shoulder. "I didn't mean to scare you." I hadn't even noticed her hand move to touch me.

I planted my boots down, shoulder width apart, and took a deep breath. "It's not you, sweetheart. It's this place. I only remember these stairs we just walked up, and that swing. It's what's inside that has me tangled up. It's loss, tragedy and an oppressive feeling of malevolence all hidden behind the face of an evil clown."

"Clown?"

I shrugged. "I hate clowns."

"Okay, an evil, malevolent clown. Is the swing a good memory or a bad memory?"

I closed my eyes. I remembered Grady sitting in the swing and smiled. "Good, definitely good."

Marlowe grabbed my big hand in her dainty one and tugged me toward the swing.

"I'm glad you like the swing, because this is my favorite part of the house. Chaos loves it out here too, especially in the evenings, after it has cooled off."

She arranged it so that I sat down first, then she sat down almost twelve inches away from me. I wasn't having any of that. I pulled her closer. As soon as I did, all feeling of ants faded.

"You feeling better?" Marlowe asked.

"How could I not be?" And wasn't that the truth? Not only were the ants gone, but a feeling of calmness enfolded me. Then she turned. Her breast brushed against my chest. I could see down the front of her dress and got a view of the prettiest breasts I'd ever seen in my whole life. Now I wasn't calm, now I was aroused. Again.

"One night you should sit here with Chaos and me," Marlowe said as she smiled up at me.

I hummed in agreement. I looked down the street. This time the dogwood trees weren't bothering me at all; as a matter of fact, I liked them. Even the one here in Marlowe's yard.

Marlowe's yard. That's how I was going to think of this place from now on.

"Lettie lives right down the street." Marlowe pointed. "There."

Did she know that her breast was brushing against me even more? I looked down. Her face was red again as she tried to pull away. *Yep, she noticed.* I kept her close to my side.

"Sorry," she mumbled.

"For what? Honey, haven't you figured out yet that I want to get to know you better? And that includes touching you?"

"But I don't want you to think I was doing that on purpose."

"All you have to do is tell me you weren't, and I'll believe you. I'll be sad, but I'll believe you."

A little giggle popped out of her mouth. "Sad?"

"Big time sad. I'm hoping one day to have a whole hell of a lot of you pressed up against me."

Her eyes got wide. "But this is our first date," she squeaked out.

God, she was adorable.

I gave her a squeeze. "Us guys, we operate this way. We make our decisions pretty quick. A woman who fits in our arms, has a pretty smile, smells good, and is interested in us, will usually do it for us."

"That's not true," she protested.

"Well, okay, it is when you're seventeen. Now, when you hit twenty, it's the same criteria, only you want to make sure she puts out."

Marlowe pushed against my chest so that she could look up at me, eyebrow raised. "Are you saying you weren't looking for girls to put out when you were seventeen?"

"I was absolutely looking for that when I was seventeen, but there were only so many girls who would put out at that age, and if you weren't on the varsity squad, you probably weren't getting yourself some. But by the time you're twenty, it's a co-ed free-for-all."

"And when is the next big milestone?" she asked me.

"Twenty-five. That seems to be when all the guys who came from functional families wanted to get married, and marry a woman like their mom."

Marlowe winced.

"Yeah, a lot of times it was a problem. The guys never asked their dad what qualities their mom had. Instead they looked at their mom through a child's lens. Often times they ended up marrying a really good housekeeper, who picked up after them, cooked their meals and didn't let him step a foot out of line. When in actuality, his dad might have married a lawyer who did nothing but pro bono work, and he loved her gentle soul. I've seen marriages like that crash and burn."

"You've really thought this through, haven't you?" Marlowe snuggled closer to my side.

"Yeah. In my unit, we would be called out of the country at a moment's notice. Anybody who was married couldn't tell their wife where they were going, how long they would be gone or when they would be back. Occasionally, we could sneak in a phone call, but that would be it. I've watched marriages implode under these circumstances, but I've seen some of my friends choose right, and their marriages are rock solid."

She was quiet for a moment, while I could hear my heart beating. Finally, she asked, "Is that what you want?"

I huffed out a laugh. "Before I was injured the thought of getting married was always something to do in the future. I was having fun on my leaves, doing stuff with my friends. Mountain climbing, base jumping. My team got invited to surf at Cape Solander, so that was fun."

Marlowe's eyes grew round. "Was there a possibility of death with all of these things?"

"Not for a person who knew what they were doing." I grinned.

She giggled. But then, she grew serious. "Are you okay knowing you might not be able to do those things after your injuries?"

Her concern touched me. How many women would ask such a thoughtful question?

"Marlowe, I've got to be. I refuse to live my life pissing and moaning about something I can't change. That's just plain stupid."

"Makes sense." Then that humorous spark returned to her eyes. "So tell me, oh wise one, what does a man look for in his thirties?"

"A man will always look for a woman who fits in his arms and smells good. Those are must-haves. So is a pretty smile that goes all the way to her eyes. In your thirties you should be smart enough to know that if you marry someone who is kind, you'll have a partner who consistently acts with integrity and compassion. Plus, they'll be caring and considerate during the good and bad times. And for fuck's sake, you need to have someone intelligent."

Marlowe let out a huge laugh. "Are you saying that not everyone you've dated has been intelligent?"

I shrugged, considering my next words. "There have been one or two who haven't been too bright, but they were by no means stupid. But some of the guys in my unit continually date a woman based on their looks and other skills, and I'm pretty sure these women's IQs are in the double digits. It's either that, or they have just lost too many brain cells doing shots at the Ramada Inn bars."

Marlowe shoved her face into my chest to stifle her giggles. God, that felt good. This whole day had felt good.

Damn good.

She pushed back again when she got her laughter under control and looked up at me. God, she was perfect. I curled my fingers and tucked them under her chin to gently lift it.

"Do you know what else a man in his thirties does?" I asked her.

"No, what?"

"He doesn't miss opportunities when they present themselves."

"Huh?"

She was genuinely perplexed. *So cute.*

I lifted her chin even higher with two knuckles, pleased when I saw her lips part.

"I want to kiss you, Marlowe Jones."

"Oh." Her brown eyes widened, and she smiled. "Yes, please."

I had never had a sweeter invitation. I lowered my head and brushed my lips against hers, slowly, softly. She sighed, and I pressed just a little harder, reveling in the soft feel of her plump lips. That electrical spark that I'd felt when we'd first shook hands was back, only stronger.

I cupped the side of her jaw with one hand, and speared my fingers through the thick, silky hair at the nape of her neck. She purred. It was a heady sound that swirled around my entire body, ending in my groin. I licked against the seam of her lips, and she opened for me. I took immediate advantage, plunging my tongue in, basking in her warm heat.

Her tongue shyly played with mine, and I pulled her closer. My hand stroked down her jaw to her neck. Her pulse fluttered like a hummingbird. I wanted to kiss her there, but later. My hand moved down farther, and soon encountered those barely there straps. I so wanted to push them down.

I played with the shoulder straps as I continued to revel in the sweetest kiss of my life. Then I started to push the strap downward, off her shoulder.

Marlowe broke our kiss and pulled away from me. If she hadn't looked as bereft as I felt I would have been upset. Instead, I was confused.

"What?" I asked.

She nodded behind me.

I looked over my shoulder and damn near swallowed my tongue.

For fuck's sake.

We were in full view of all her neighbors and any car that happened to be driving down the street. When was the last time I was so unaware of my environment? Had I lost every part of being Delta after that sniper attack?

I pushed back Marlowe's straps and slowly pulled my fingers out of her hair. It had to be slow, because it felt so good. I was reluctant to look into her eyes, but when I did, all I saw was dazed wonder. Add to that her swollen lips and her flushed cheeks, and I felt like I was ten feet tall.

"I'm sorry," we both said at the same time.

"Let me go first," I said when she opened her mouth to continue. She nodded. "I shouldn't have gotten carried away like that on your front porch. My only excuse is that you're absolutely gorgeous and I've been thinking about kissing you since I saw you outside the Whispering Pines Inn."

"You were?" She asked, her voice breathy.

"I was. I definitely was."

"That's nice."

I grinned. She made me grin a lot.

"You could come inside, I could get you some lemonade or something," she offered.

"I get the feeling that's all that's on offer. Am I right?"

She nodded.

"Normally, I would say yes, but I'm not ready to face the inside of this house quite yet. Can I get a raincheck?"

She nodded again.

"You're awfully accommodating." I noted.

"You just gave me the best kiss of my life, why wouldn't I be accommodating?"

"Does that mean you're willing to go out with me again?"

Marlowe gave a slow smile. "We just agreed I was accommodating, didn't we?"

"Yes. Yes we did. But I get a feeling, you're only accommodating on the things you want to be accommodating about."

"That's true. Now," she muttered. Suddenly she wasn't smiling or looking at me.

"Is there a story there?"

She bit her lip. "It's a tenth date story." She looked me in the eyes. "Kind of like parts of your childhood are a tenth date story, you know?"

Ouch. "That bad, huh?"

She nodded and pushed up off the swing. I missed the feel of her body immediately.

"Is our date over?" I asked, hoping the answer was no.

"I have to take Chaos for a walk."

I wondered if it was my reluctance to go inside with her, or if I'd somehow touched a nerve when I asked her about her past. She'd dodged my attempts to ask her about herself at the diner as well.

She headed for her front door, but I caught up to her and touched her hand. No way was I leaving things ambiguous. She turned around.

"Since you promised me a tenth date, how soon can we have a second date?"

Marlowe smiled. "School still hasn't started. I'm working on lesson plans, but I don't have specific hours I have to work, so call me and we can set something up."

Still too ambiguous.

"Expect a call tomorrow."

Mercifully, her smile got bigger. "I will."

11

"So how did it go?"

"Uhm, good." I set my phone on the kitchen island, pulled down a wine glass, and grabbed a good bottle of Oregon Riesling out of the fridge that I had been saving for a special occasion. And this sure was an occasion.

"Am I hearing you tearing foil off a bottle of wine?" Sue always had had bat-like hearing.

"Maybe," I muttered. I found my corkscrew in my newly minted junk drawer and popped the cork.

"Why do you need wine?"

I poured my glass and thought about how to answer Sue's question.

"Girl! Talk to me. You're killing me here! Say something."

I took a large sip. Okay, it was a gulp.

"It went well."

"It went well. Sure it did," Sue said sarcastically.

"That's the reason you're chugging wine at four o'clock in the afternoon. Don't ask me how I know. I heard that gulp. Now talk to me. What's the problem?"

I took another gulp of the golden goodness. It helped calm my nerves.

"I like him. That's the problem. Okay? I like him. But he seemed too nice. Too kind. Even when he was nervous because he wanted information about his brother, his nervousness was too perfect. It wasn't right. All of this was after he volunteered to help some stroke victim he'd never met. Sue, I really like Kai, but after Denny, I just can't trust my own opinion. And I sure as hell can't trust some guy who seems too perfect. That got me into trouble the first time around. Denny was just luring me in for the kill."

After all that word vomit, I picked up my glass and sucked down the rest of the wine.

"Have you finished your glass?" Sue asked gently.

"Yes." I gave the phone a dirty look. "And I'm thinking about pouring another one."

"Before you do, can we have a calm, back and forth conversation?"

"How long?"

"Less than five minutes, I promise."

I started the timer on my phone. "The clock has started."

"I hate it when you do that," Sue complained.

"You're wasting your time."

"Fine. Denny spent four months being perfect before he asked you to move in with him. He never wanted to meet any of your friends. He wanted to isolate you from everyone. He was an antisocial asshole. Is that Kai?"

"It was one date. How would I know?"

"Somebody must have talked him into helping this man who had a stroke," Sue prompted.

"We were surrounded by people from the town. There was Lettie the waitress at the diner, then Harvey. I told you about him, I think. He owns the local construction company. I met him and his wife at Lettie's potluck. That man can eat. Then there was the town doctor, who everybody calls Doc."

Sue laughed.

"So was Kai there amongst everyone?"

"Yeah."

"Did he seem fidgety?"

I thought about it. "He didn't seem to. He really wasn't fidgeting when it was just me and him and Lettie. He was charming and funny. He was really nice to Little Grandma, too."

"Ohh," Sue sighed. "You've told me about her. I think I'm going to bring Steve and Angie out for a visit just so I can meet Little Grandma."

"You better be coming to visit me."

"And Chaos."

I laughed. "And Chaos."

"So Kai is actually good with people. That's not the same as Denny."

I felt my shoulders relax. "You're right."

"What did you talk about with Mr. Perfect?"

"It was weird, Sue. After everybody left, Kai made me feel like I was the most important person in the universe. He listened to me. Really listened."

"As he should have. And what did you talk about?"

"We talked about his brother Beau, of course."

"Of course."

"He wanted to know what I knew about him, and I explained I didn't know much, but how grateful I was that he seemed to care enough about Chaos that it was okay for me to install a doggie door for her. I also told him that Beau insisted on paying for it as a modification for his house."

"What did he think about that?"

"He was okay with it, I guess."

"And?"

I really wanted another glass before I started talking about Kai's near-death experience.

Fuck it.

"Are you pouring yourself another glass of wine?"

"Yes I am. Get over it. I need one." I took a sip, not a gulp, and started talking. "Kai told me how he got injured. They thought he was going to die. He had multiple surgeries on his neck in Germany, then they sent him to Walter Reed in the states. He stayed there for eight months. They told him he wouldn't walk. He sure proved them wrong."

"God, Marlowe. I don't know what to say."

"I know, right? Then he told me how his bastard

of a father had him working on those dangerous crab boats out in the Alaska ocean when he was ten years old."

"No way."

I nodded, then realized she couldn't see me. "Really. Ten years old. His father was evil, Sue. Pure evil. But at least some of the crew was watching out for him."

This time when I took a gulp of wine, Sue didn't give me any shit.

"I asked him if anything good happened after he started working on the boat, and he told me about this one time that some of the crew members took him on a flight to a place called Sitka, and they saw some fjords. He made them sound magical."

"You mean like in Norway?"

"Yes, with glaciers. Anyway, they also took him regular fishing, like with a rod and reel."

"How sweet. That's incredible that they did that." Sue sighed. That's why we were such good friends. When I had been busy hardening my shell after Denny, Sue was there to add big poofs of emotional cotton candy to my life. I pressed off the timer.

"Yeah, it was."

"But Kai did do one kind of Denny thing. He looked at me whenever I drank my sweet tea. He would get all intense and stare. I've never felt so self-conscious sucking on a straw before."

Sue's laughter rang through my phone.

"What?"

"He was so imagining you sucking his dick."

"What?" I screeched.

"You heard me. Every time you sucked on your straw, he was imagining you sucking his dick."

"He was not."

"Was too."

"Was not," I shot back.

"When I really want to mess with Steve when we're out for dinner, I start playing with my straw and take my time sucking on it as I drink. It's really good if it's a milkshake with whip cream. His eyes practically roll back in his head."

"You, Sue Rankin, are a dirty girl."

"And I fly that flag high and proud."

I couldn't stop the laugh that came straight from my belly. Okay, there were a zillion reasons why Sue was my best friend. Her being a dirty girl was a zillion-and-one.

"And then if you really want to mess with them, take the straw out of the milkshake, scoop up some of the whipped cream with the end of your straw, then lick it off with the tip of your tongue. That's like the dirty triple word score."

I laughed even harder, imagining lumberjack-sized Steve Rankin wrapped around tiny little Sue Rankin's finger.

"Now tell me more about the date," my friend demanded.

"Can't. Laughing too hard," I gasped.

I pushed up from the kitchen island and stood up

straight. Sue was absolutely right. Why hadn't I seen that? "Sue, you are a genius."

"I'm a dirty-girl genius," she said smugly.

"He kissed me."

"Whaaaatttt?!" Sue screeched.

"It was magnificent."

"Where? When? How long? Was there tongue?"

"On my front porch swing. After the date. Long enough for me to lose my mind. Yes, there was tongue. And he wants to go out again."

"When? What are you going to wear? Do you need to go shopping? You could Facetime me from the dressing room."

"Whoa. I didn't tell him yes, yet. I told him to call me."

"Yuck. That sounds like you're playing games."

"Well, I'm not." *At least not anymore.* "I just needed to get my head on straight, and you helped. So, thank you."

"Anytime."

"I'm hanging up now."

"Remember to call me so we can go video shopping together."

"I won't forget."

12

"Enjoying yourself much?"

I looked out the left side mirror and laughed as I saw Chaos' tongue lolling out of her mouth and the amount of drool that was hitting the side of my 4Runner. Thank God Sue's husband had turned me onto Groits Garage car care products. That stuff took six hundred miles of bug goo off my windshield and everything else. A little bit of Chaos drool was nothing.

"Isn't that right, girl?"

She ignored me. She was liking this road. I was too. Well, kind of. It was a little steep for me, but that's what you got when you were living in the Smoky Mountains. I looked behind me again, making sure I wasn't holding anyone up. That was one of my biggest fears. The last thing I needed was someone tailgating me on this narrow two-lane highway.

Nope. Nothing.

I turned up the radio, and when Bonnie Raitt's song, "Let's Give Them Something to Talk About" came on, I turned it up *real* loud. That's what Kai and I had been doing in Jasper Creek for the last three weeks. People were really talking about us.

I actually saw a woman with purple hair point at me. Point. With her finger. Then she said to the lady she was standing next to in the post office line that I had been kissing Grady Beaumont on his front porch.

"Florence, get your story straight. She wasn't kissing Grady. Grady is Beau, and he's still not home from the service. She was kissing Brady." That came from the man behind the post office counter.

Normally I would have wanted the floor to swallow me up, but I was too amazed by all their knowledge.

"Brady doesn't like to be called Brady," the woman at the front of the line said. "He calls hisself, Kai. What kind of name is Kai, anyway?"

The lady behind me tapped me on the shoulder. "Honey, is he going to be staying in town, or is he going back to where he came from?"

"I don't know." I answered.

"That's a shame," she said. "Try to get him to stay."

Then everyone chimed in about how sad they would be to see Brady leave.

Yep, we were definitely giving the town something to talk about. I started singing along with Bonnie.

Woof!

Woof!

Why was—

Wham!

Something hit me from behind hard enough that I jolted forward against my seatbelt then whipped backwards.

Owwww!

God, that hurt. I tried to get my shit together, but the pain in my head and neck was shorting out my brain. My rearview mirror showed me a huge truck falling behind me as I sped forward.

Wait!

"Chaos!"

Nothing.

"Chaos! Answer me!"

I heard her whining. I couldn't see her on the seat, so I figured she must be on the floor. She sounded pitiful, but at least I knew she was alive.

"Thank you, Jesus."

But we had a bigger problem. I was now in the oncoming traffic lane and if I didn't do something about it, we were both goners. At least we were on a stretch of straight road but that was going to change a quarter-mile ahead, where the road curved to the right around the rock-wall side of the mountain. I jerked the wheel to put us back into the correct lane just as a car appeared around the sharp curve. The driver honked and flashed their headlights at me as they passed. I hit the brake to slow down for the curve and still took it too fast when—

Crunch!

Something hit us again from behind after we cleared the curve. Not as hard this time, thank God. My foot was on the brake but I was picking up speed. That made no sense.

What the hell?

Chaos kept whining from the back seat, terrified or possibly hurt. I looked in the rearview mirror to see what had hit me. It took a moment to decipher what I was seeing, because it looked like just a big slab of black with a shiny grill. I blinked. Then blinked again. It was the truck that had been behind me earlier, hitting me a second time. Not a semi, more like a Ford One Thousand or something. It was right against my back bumper, pushing me.

Why?

Maybe the driver was having a seizure or a heart attack.

The truck pushed me back into the oncoming traffic lane. I was going to have a head-on collision and end up accordioned between the truck and God knew what other vehicle.

What is happening? People could die!

I honked my horn. Then I just leaned on it, trying to warn any cars that might be coming around the next bend—this one about half a mile ahead—while I tried to figure out what to do.

I craned my head out my window and turned to get a look at the driver.

He grinned at me.

Holy hell. He wanted me to die.

If I didn't have a head-on collision, then he was going to shove me into the flimsy looking guardrails and right off the cliff.

Think!

I spied my purse on the floor of the passenger side. It had my phone in it. That was it, I needed to call 911. But first I needed to stop them from pushing me. I took a deep breath. My regular brakes weren't doing any good, just burning my tires. I engaged my parking brake, and that slowed things down, but it didn't stop us. I reached down for my purse but I couldn't grab it, not with my seatbelt on.

"Fuck the seatbelt!" I yelled out.

Chaos whined again.

"It's okay, girl, I'm going to get us out of this, I promise."

I did something insane and popped the seatbelt to grab my purse.

"Got it!"

And then I almost cried when I saw that the phone had fallen out. I had no chance of reaching it before we got to the second curve.

I pulled my seatbelt back on and almost had a heart attack when I saw how close we were to the curve ahead. I threw my whole body into turning the wheel. I knew deep in my soul they were going to push me into the barrier so that I would go careening over the cliff.

Metal screamed as the side of my 4Runner kissed the barrier as I flew around the curve. The truck stayed right up against my rear.

Braking didn't work, so I did the opposite. I took off the emergency brake and started to gun it, hoping I could put a little distance between us and at least get back into the correct lane. But the other driver knew immediately what I was doing and got there first. He drew up parallel to me, then swerved. He hit the passenger side, trying to send me through the barrier again.

Chaos yelped.

I hit the accelerator again, practically pushing it through the floor. For an instant nothing happened.

Nothing.

Nothing.

Then my 4Runner jolted into life. I miraculously sped ahead of the truck, back in the right lane, but I had overshot and was close to hitting the side of the mountain. I corrected course. My clammy hands were so slippery that trying to steer was almost impossible, but at least I was now kind of in my lane as I started to race down a steeper slope. My eyes were constantly shooting between the view in front of me and my rearview mirror. I tore around another curve, losing my view of the truck. When the road straightened again I looked back.

I saw neither hide nor hair of the truck.

I never aspired to be a NASCAR driver. I never played driving games at the family fun centers, but by God, I was planning on winning a trophy today. I was almost doubling the speed limit. Nobody was going to kill my dog!

It wasn't until I fed onto Hwy 321, with no appearance of the truck, that I began to feel safe. Not calm, just a little safe.

I knew where the animal hospital was located since I'd met the vet at the grocery store one day. I drove straight to it, a block down from the hardware store, right next to the beauty parlor.

For the first time I didn't smile when I read the word 'parlor.' I was too worried about Chaos. Another miracle happened, and I found a parking spot right in front of Jasper Creek Animal Hospital. I threw open my door, slammed it, then opened the back door.

Chaos was lying on the floor on the passenger side. She lifted her head and whined. She never did that. I climbed in and crawled across the passenger seat to get to her. I tried to see what was wrong with her.

"Oh baby, I want to hug you so bad, but that might hurt you."

Woof.

It was such a soft bark that I could barely hear it.

"I'm going to go get you some help. Okay?"

I crawled backwards, got out of the car, and ran

into the vet's office. There was a nice young kid at the front desk and I immediately started talking.

"I was in a car wreck. Someone rear-ended me then hit the side of my car. Bad. My dog was in the back seat. She's not moving. I don't know what's wrong. But she needs immediate help."

The kid, who couldn't be more than twenty, bit his lip. "You don't have an appointment."

A brunette with a cat carrier came up to the desk. "Rick, go back and talk to Kizzie. You're an animal hospital. This is an emergency. She needs to know about this."

"Ms. Avery, she doesn't like it when I interrupt her when she's with a patient."

"She'll be more upset if you don't. Trust me, okay?"

The young man looked at her like she hung the moon, nodded, and went through a door to the back.

"Thank you," I told her. "I wasn't going to handle that well. Would you tell them I'm right out front? It's a green 4Runner."

"I'll tell her. She needs a stretcher, right?"

I nodded as I went outside.

I opened the other back door this time, the one near Chaos' head. I put my hand near her muzzle and she licked it. She tried to lift her head, but it seemed too much for her.

"It's okay sweetie, just rest. Kizzie will take care of you."

"Marlowe, right?"

I hadn't even heard Kizzie come up behind me, I'd been so focused on Chaos. I spun around and looked straight into Kizzie's concerned blue eyes.

"Yeah, I'm Marlowe, and this is Chaos. I got a pretty bad jolt when we were hit, and I was buckled in. Chaos wasn't buckled in, so I don't know what happened to her."

Kizzie took one look at Chaos and said, "We're going to have to get her out of the car and onto a stretcher."

13

Not for the first time, it occurred to me that Lettie must really have a close relationship with Gretchen if I was only paying three times the rate as the LeeHy motel and getting this phenomenal suite at the Whispering Pines Inn. For God's sake, it had a desk and comfortable rolling chair, and there was a couch and coffee table along with a nice-sized walk-in shower and a soaking tub that I could actually fit in. I'd questioned Gretchen twice, and she said that it was part of the owner's guidelines. Whenever possible, put members of the armed services in the nicest accommodations possible.

The second time I clarified, she told me the same thing, so I just shrugged and asked her to relay my thanks. Then I went back to my room to do some online searching to see what I could find out about the owners. Turned out the hotel was partially owned by a development company out of Nashville, but the main owner was a company named O'Malley Enterprises that operated out of San Diego. I dug a little deeper and found that the officers of the company were a husband and wife, Aiden O'Malley and Evalyn O'Malley. Aiden was a Lieutenant of a Navy SEAL team out of Coronado and Evalyn's maiden name was Avery and she was born and raised here in Jasper Creek.

It wasn't the first time that I ran into someone in the service who had family money, but this was some serious coin if the man could afford to be the major investor in this hotel. Not that I was complaining. This was a sweet deal, especially since I didn't know how long I was going to be in town.

I got up from my chair and did some stretches. Yep, I'd been sitting too long. Probably time for a walk or a ride. I also needed to see if I could get in touch with the elusive Bernie Faulks. Voicemails and e-mails didn't seem to work. According to Lettie and Pearl, who were my primary sources of information, Bernie was basically a hermit, even if he had gotten hitched. Their word, not mine.

I'd asked who he'd married, but they'd clammed up. Said if they'd given me her information and I'd tried to reach Bernie through his wife, there'd be hell to pay.

Interesting guy.

They did give me the coordinates to his cabin. I had to chuckle at that. Seemed that the man really was off the grid if I was getting latitude and longitude instead of an address. But I had to say I preferred it that way. More precise.

I got into my hiking clothes and made sure that I was kitted out to find someone. The idea of hunting someone down felt good.

Real good.

When I went downstairs, Roberta was at the desk. She straight-up reminded me of Peg Bundy—lots of make-up, red hair teased high—but without the cigarettes the *Married with Children* character smoked constantly.

"Hey, Doll, how you doing?"

"I'm doing fine, Roberta. How are the kids?"

"My little darlins are driving me up a wall. Was so glad that Gretchen called me in for a shift today. Before she handed over the keys, she handed me a pan of fresh-baked peanut-butter cookies with chocolate chunks. I don't suppose you'd want any?"

"I don't know, would you kill me if I took any from you?" I teased.

"I might. Let's see how it goes."

She held out the pan. I snatched three before she could pull the pan back.

"Dammit, Kai. That was not a nice thing to do."

"What, were you planning on giving them to your kids?"

"Hell no. I was going to eat them for breakfast, mid-morning snack, and then lunch."

"Not dinner?"

"There weren't going to be any left for dinner.

The only reason I offered them to you is I like how you fill out a t-shirt."

"Ro, if only you weren't married to a man who could take me out with one punch, I'd take you away from all of this and make you mine."

"As if. Rumor has it that you're spending time with our new math teacher. Heard you took her to Gatlinburg for the all-important third date. How'd that go?" Roberta waggled her eyebrows.

"A gentleman never tells." Even if Marlowe and I booked a hotel for a night in Gatlinburg so that nobody would notice my truck outside her house for the night, or her truck outside this place for the night, somebody from here would still report I hadn't come back here for the night. I was going to have to talk to Marlowe about this on Thursday when she was making me dinner.

"How 'bout I offer you two more cookies?"

"Huh?" I'd lost the plot.

"If you tell me if you and Marlowe slept together, I'll give you two more cookies."

"Nope, not going to do it. Anyway, I've got to get going. I'm heading up the mountain."

"Okay, Doll. You be safe."

"Always."

I chuckled to myself at her words. 'Be careful.' Hell yes. 'Be safe.' Well, that was always a crap shoot. But my team was good. Damn good. I really needed to check in with some of the other guys besides Clay.

Now that my mood was looking up, I felt up to talking to them.

I threw my gear into the back of the truck and climbed into the driver's seat. I took the road that Lettie had told me to take and ended up at a small cabin. Looking at the dirt around the front steps, nobody had been there for a while. But I had to smile at the painted rocks that decorated each of the steps that led up to the porch. I wouldn't have thought the place would have been big enough for a family to have lived here.

I shrugged. Not my business. I grabbed my pack out of the back of my truck and shrugged it onto my shoulders. It felt great that now that I was allowed to carry forty pounds. I really didn't need forty pounds of gear, but I wanted the exercise. I looked around and saw a definite path into the woods so I took it. Soon I was in a different time and space, and I was loving it.

I'd grown up around the ocean. Then after joining the Army, there were times I could sit and be surrounded by the quiet of a massive desert. I had trudged through jungles for months on end, and still there were times I could look past the heat and bugs and see the lush beauty. But this? This forest with the sun sparkling down through the trees, was glorious. Every sight, smell, and sound immersed me in bliss.

When I was thirty meters away from my target, I stopped before I would've lost my forest camouflage. There was about twenty meters of clear-cut around the front and both sides of the two-story A-frame with a deck out front. Smart. I wondered whether it was to help with forest fires, or to let him see who was coming toward him. I needed to check if the clear-cut extended to the back of the house as well.

Ten years of training was a hard thing to let go of, so I took out the binoculars that really weren't that expensive but had all the bells and whistles I wanted. I took my time doing my reconnaissance. I went all around the property, and by the time I made it around to the south side, I smelled beef grilling.

I returned to where I started and watched Bernie Faulkes turn three steaks over and put three foil-wrapped potatoes onto the grill. I also clocked a rifle leaning up against the side of the house that hadn't been there before. I took note of the Bowie knife strapped to his belt.

"Are we eating out here, or inside?" A woman called out from inside.

"We'll ask our guest, but my guess is he'd feel more comfortable eating outside."

Might as well show myself now, before their guest showed up. I stepped out of the forest and into the clearing.

"Hello," I hollered.

"Hey," Bernie hollered back as I continued to walk toward his house. "Are you Kai Davies? Beau's brother?"

"That'd be me," I answered as I stood at the bottom of his stairs to his deck.

"Well, come on up. Been waiting for you. Hope you like steak."

"I do like steak."

"How do you like it cooked?"

"Medium rare."

Bernie chuckled. "Then you made it in time." He turned back to the grill and took off two of the steaks and put them on a plate.

An attractive middle-aged woman with a silver bob stepped out on the deck, carrying a salad bowl. "What kind of dressing do you like on your salad?"

"Oh wait, Mora, I didn't ask him if he wanted to eat inside or outside. So, which is it, Kai?" Bernie asked.

"Outside. It's going to be a beautiful evening."

Mora settled the bowl in the middle of the table, then she went back inside.

"I suppose you want to talk about Beau. Am I right?" Bernie asked as he poked the baked potatoes with a fork.

"You're right. Not only do I want any information you might feel comfortable sharing, what I'd like most is for you to set up a FaceTime call between us."

Bernie nodded at his grill. "Not surprised. Last time I talked to him, he and his team were in Eastern Europe. He shouldn't have told me that much, but I think he wanted me to know that this mission was ugly. But he was fighting the good fight."

I frowned. No American troops should be fighting in Eastern Europe. As a member of Delta

Force I knew that it was our job to be invisible and do things that nobody else should or could do. But Beau was a Marine, he wouldn't be doing that...

"What does he do in the Marine Corps?"

Bernie looked over his shoulder at me, taking his time to answer. "Raider."

Well, that explained that. My brother might not be Delta, but being a Marine Raider was definitely in the ballpark.

"Now sit down for dinner, then we can talk about Beau."

———

I liked how Bernie and Mora were together. Nothing overt, but she would touch his shoulder, and he would reach out and squeeze her hand. Then there was the way that they could finish one another's sentences. I'd gotten the feeling from Lettie that they'd only been together for a couple of years, but they acted like a couple who had been together for decades.

"If you don't like any of the dressings," Mora pointed to the three bottles she'd brought out, "I can whip up a something tangy with the balsamic vinegar I have inside."

"I'm a blue cheese man, so this definitely works." I snagged the bottle from the middle of the table and poured some onto my salad.

"How are you liking things over at the Whispering Pines?" Bernie asked.

"Great. Actually, wonderful."

Bernie and Mora both laughed. "You started out at the LeeHy, didn't you?" Mora asked. "I heard that Derek checked you in." She gave a delicate shudder.

"Yep," I sighed. "I heard his parents tried with him, but it didn't stick."

"Lovely people. I had him in a couple of my middle school classes. He struggled."

Bernie snorted. "I imagine he did."

"Bernard, we don't need you starting in on that poor boy," Mora admonished.

I looked at Bernie and raised my eyebrow. His glance back at me made it clear that only Mora was allowed to call him Bernard. I gave him a chin tilt, and went back to my loaded baked potato.

"I hear from Beau every so often. We don't have a set time or anything," Bernie said after he finished his salad.

"More lemonade?" Mora asked.

"How about a beer? Would you like one?" Bernie asked me.

I nodded.

"I can—"

"Sit down." Bernie smiled as he put his hand on Mora's shoulder. "Do you want more lemonade, Darlin'?"

"Yes please."

"Coming right up."

Mora looked at me closely. "You are the spitting image of your brother."

"Are you on the FaceTime calls?"

"I've been on two. I taught him when he was younger. He was always such a quiet and somber boy. He only had two friends. I would specifically create group projects so that Beau would have to interact with more than his two friends, but he never really opened up. He always ended up the team leader, and made sure the others did their part, but he was never social."

"Was that because of his moth— I mean, our mother?"

"I think it was partly because of his mother, but he was also missing you."

She noticed my frown.

"What is it, Kai?"

"I'm just wondering why he remembered me and I didn't remember him. That doesn't make any sense."

"You've got to remember, it was a big deal when Arthur kidnapped you. The police were at your house, there were neighbors bringing meals and coming in to babysit Grady and support Rose, because she broke down. It made quite an impact on little Grady. What's more, he was still injured from the beating he'd received from Arthur, so he needed extra care. All of that had to have made an impression."

"Are you telling Kai about when he was kidnapped?" Bernie asked as he set down the lemonade pitcher in front of her and handed a long-neck to me and set another one at his place setting. "Here's the bottle opener, but you being Special Operations, I'm assuming you could open this with your teeth." Bernie laughed.

"Special Operations?" I frowned. "Why do you say that?"

"You have that look about you. Same as Beau."

"If I had been Spec Ops, those days are long gone," I said as I used the bottle opener on the beer. I handed it back to Bernie. He gave me a chin tilt then opened his beer and took a swallow. The man still had a shit-eating grin on his face. I wasn't fooling him one damn bit.

"I had a feeling you'd be stopping by soon. I sent him a message on WhatsApp that I needed to get in touch with him. Beau has an iPhone and he uses FaceTime because of the security. Do you have an iPhone?"

I nodded.

"Give me your number so that I can have him call you. His number is going to come to you as blocked. You'll know it's him by the time he's calling."

I set down my knife and fork and looked at Bernie. "I can't tell you how much I appreciate this."

"I've also talked to Nash Rivers, our sheriff. He doesn't think that there is a kidnapping case to be made against your dad. There's the time factor, and the fact that Arthur and your mom weren't split up."

"I really didn't want to have to deal with Arthur

or Ronald ever again. Good-bye to bad rubbish as one of my teammates used to say. Last I saw him, life was looking pretty miserable for him. Made me happy."

"Not as happy as Mora's strawberry rhubarb cobbler is going to make you. You got any of that special vanilla ice cream? The bean kind?" Bernie was looking like a hopeful puppy.

"I do. Kai, are you ready for cobbler?"

"I am."

I watched Bernie watching Mora as she went into the cabin. He turned back to me. He started to say something when my phone rang. I saw it was Marlowe, so I answered.

"Hi, Sweetheart. What's going on?"

"Chaos is in surgery. When a car tried to run me off the road, Chaos was knocked around in the backseat," she paused. I heard her take in a deep breath, but it was full of tears. "She broke at least one rib and it punctured her lung. Kizzie told me to stay strong."

"Kizzie?"

"The vet here in town. She's the one operating on her. If you're not busy, could you...?" Her voice trailed off.

"Marlowe, I'll be there as quick as I can. I'm at Bernie Faulke's house. He lives up the mountain. I hiked in. It'll take me a little bit to get to you. But I'll get there as fast as I can. I'm calling Lettie right now, so she can come and sit with you."

"No, that's all right, I'm fine."

I could hear the wobble in her voice. Of course she would say she was fine. She always said she was fine.

"Hang tight for me, Sweetheart, okay?"

"I will," she whispered.

When I hung up my phone, Bernie was standing close, holding out a set of keys.

"What are those?"

"The keys to your ATV. You're going to be following me off the mountain. There are roads, you just need to know where to find them, is all."

I nodded.

"Let me make one phone call, then let's get going."

I called Lettie.

14

I parked the ATV in the hardware store parking lot. It was as close to the animal hospital as I could get. Bernie was close behind me. I ran up to the door, but before I could open it, I stopped, because I saw Marlowe's 4Runner. The backend was beat to shit. So was the passenger side.

What the fuck?

Bernie came up behind me.

"Does this 4Runner belong to Marlowe?" he asked.

"Yep. And it wasn't looking like this two days ago. Looks like someone rear-ended her. More than once. Sideswiped her, too."

Furious, I turned and went into the animal hospital. As soon as I opened the door, I saw Nash Rivers, Lettie, Alice Draper, and some guy I didn't know. Nash and the guy were hovering over Marlowe who was seated. I could tell she'd been crying. As soon as she saw me, she leaped up. I pushed my way between the two men and pulled her into my arms.

"Any news?"

"She's been in surgery for over an hour," she whispered into my shoulder. "Kizzie said it was bad when she examined her. Kai, I'm afraid she's going to die."

She started to cry.

I looked over my shoulder at Nash.

"Marlowe said someone was trying to run her off the road. Amber Road. Up near the Slurry slope."

I squeezed her harder. I couldn't help it. If they had succeeded, she would have gone over the steep side of the mountain.

I turned us around, so I was facing Nash and the other guy. "Any idea who did it?"

"All I could tell them was it was a big, black truck with two men in it," Marlowe whispered into my chest.

"I have one of my deputies up there looking around," Nash told me. "We'll also be taking paint samples from the back of Marlowe's 4Runner."

"Can you explain to us again who you think tried to run you off the road?" Nash asked. For the first time I noticed he had a notepad in his hands.

"It seems farfetched, but I'm suing my old principal for wrongful termination. I can't imagine that she would be so upset that she would want me dead. That's the only person I can think of who would want me dead."

"Any old boyfriends?"

Marlowe pulled out of my arms. I didn't like it, but I had to deal with it. "The last man I had in my life didn't take it well when I left. But it was four years ago."

"What do you mean, he didn't take it well?" Nash asked the question I wanted answered.

"He sent me notes and followed me around. Stuff like that."

"When did he stop doing that?"

Marlowe didn't answer for a long time. "After I got a restraining order," she finally admitted. I could hear the quaver in her voice.

I pulled Marlowe back into my arms.

"Marlowe, you didn't file an order of protection with me when you came into town. That is one of the first things you should have done when you arrived."

"It's been four years," Marlowe protested.

"Did you let the restraining order lapse while you were in West Virginia?" Nash continued.

She shook her head. "But that's because the officer working my case would call me and remind me to re-file."

Me, Nash, and the other guy all exchanged pointed glances. If the cop was doing that then there were definitely more things going on than just calls and him occasionally following her. Out of the corner of my eye, I could see that Lettie and Alice were listening in.

They'd want to provide emotional support to

Marlowe, but there wasn't a chance in hell I would let her out of my sight any time soon.

"What city in West Virginia did you file the restraining order, and what was the name of the officer who was handling your case?"

"Danville, Officer Tom Grant." We all heard the reluctance in her voice.

"Sheriff, I'll want to know what you hear from Officer Grant."

"That's not your purview," Nash protested.

I raised my eyebrow, then nodded toward Marlowe. Nash tilted his head, and I knew I would be hearing what was in the report.

"Me too," the other guy said.

"What's your name?" I asked. I wasn't nice about it.

"I'm Simon Clark. I run a security company here in town."

"Why would a town this small need a sheriff's office *and* a security company?"

"We work nationwide," Simon replied. "You're retired spec ops, right?"

I frowned. How in the hell did everybody know that? First Bernie, now this guy. I gave a small nod.

He pulled out his wallet and drew out a card.

Simon Clark
Security

There was no address, just a phone number.

"Give me a call. I had planned to call you, but this makes things easier."

"I'm not planning to stay around. Just want to connect with my brother."

Marlowe softly whimpered. It was so soft I barely heard it. But I did.

Dammit.

"Understood," Simon said with a smile. "How's the physical therapy going with Sam?"

I was beginning to hate this town. Seriously, did everybody know everything?

"It's going fine."

"Give me a call," Simon said with a smile. He turned to Nash. "E-mail me anything you get from Officer Grant. I want in on this."

"Won't that be up to Marlowe?" Nash asked.

"It's a freebie. Nobody fucks with people in my town." Simon tipped his chin to Nash and me. "Marlowe, you call Trenda if you need anything, alright?"

"I will," she said. She was still speaking to my chest. I liked it.

Nash pulled out his phone and started talking. It must have been on vibrate. "Okay, I'll come outside." He looked at me. "My guy is outside, ready to investigate Marlowe's 4Runner. I'll let you know what I find out."

I nodded.

"Marlowe, it was smart thinking, what you did up on that mountain," Nash said. "You saved your life. And your dog's."

She whimpered. "But she might not live," she said as she pushed away from my chest to look up at the sheriff.

"It was because of your quick thinking that Chaos has a chance. Be proud of yourself." He squeezed her shoulder, then followed Simon out the door.

There was a story there, but I didn't ask. Right now, I just wanted to get Marlowe sitting down close to me, and comfort her as we waited for Chaos to get out of surgery.

I'll never know how I fell asleep in the chair, leaning against Kai's chest. It must have been the adrenaline crash.

"Marlowe. Sweetheart. Wake up."

I looked up and saw glacier-blue eyes. It took a moment for me to orient myself, and when I did, I sat straight up. Then I looked around. Kizzie was crouched down in front of me.

"Oh, God," I cried out.

"No, Marlowe. It's good news, so far. Chaos made it through the surgery with flying colors."

"Can I see her?" I stood up, and so did Kizzie.

"Absolutely, but first I want to tell you the next steps. We're going to keep her here for probably a week. We need to monitor her vital signs and hydrate her with intravenous fluids."

I nodded. I was only halfway listening, I wanted

to see my baby. Kizzie must have noticed, because she put her hand on my shoulder.

"Marlowe, when she's released to you, there's going to be a lot of other things that you're going to do, like—"

"Kizzie, can we go over this later? I just want to see Chaos." Kai was standing beside me, his arm around my waist. Kizzie smiled.

"Sure, but she's still sedated."

"I don't care. I just want to watch her breathe."

"Come on back."

I followed Kizzie back. She led me into a room where I saw Chaos had an oxygen mask on and an IV inserted. I wanted to cry again, but I wasn't going to. These were good things. I went over to her and started to pet her behind her ears, just the way she liked. I put my lips really close to her ear.

"I love you, honey. I'm here for you. Pretty soon you'll get to come home with me, and I'll make you lots of yummy food, and I'll get to pet you, and we'll watch TV together. We'll watch *World of the Wild* again. You like that show, remember?"

I thought I felt her ear flick, but it was probably my imagination. Still, I intended to visit her every day that she was recuperating.

"I love you, Chaos. Do what the doctor tells you to do, okay?"

I kissed her, then turned and saw Kai and Kizzie standing there. Both of them were smiling.

"Come on, Marlowe, let's get you home," Kai said. "Have you ever sat on the back of an ATV?"

"I'm from West Virginia."

He grinned.

"Well, that answers that."

He held out his hand to me and I grabbed hold, tight.

"Kizzie, I can't thank you enough."

"Marlowe, this was a fantastic day as far as I'm concerned. I'll be smiling when I go to bed tonight. That's all the thanks I need."

I broke away from Kai and pulled Kizzie in for a hug.

"Well, still, thank you, from the bottom of my heart."

15

_____

I parked the ATV at the Whispering Pines and ushered Marlowe inside. Gretchen took one look at Marlowe and rushed out from behind the reception desk.

"What's wrong?"

"Marlowe got run off the road, and her dog just went through a tough surgery and is going to need to stay at the animal hospital for a week."

"Oh, honey." She looked at Marlowe, then stepped closer to her but hesitated. It was clear she wanted to hug her, but unsure if Marlowe wanted one from her.

"I could sure use a hug," she told Gretchen. Gretchen pulled her into her arms.

"I'm so sorry. Come into the restaurant. Let's get you something to eat."

I'd eaten there once, but the prices were high and the portions were small. That was the reason I always ate in town or nuked something that I'd bought at

Roger's supermarket. Gretchen ushered us both toward the restaurant, up to the hostess desk. "Matthew, give them a booth, and their bill is on the house."

Matthew nodded.

"This way."

Soon we were ensconced in a private booth, with ice water and a big basket of bread with three different kinds of spreads to put on it, but no butter. Weird.

Marlowe moved closer to me. Not quite touching, but closer.

I put my arm around her shoulder and closed the gap. Then a waiter came up to announce the specials. After the steak and baked potato, I wasn't all that hungry, so I ordered soup and salad. Marlowe did the same.

"Before you place the order with the kitchen, can you come back in five minutes?" I asked the server.

"Sure," he said.

Marlowe looked perplexed.

"Sweets, I already had a steak and baked potato for lunch, so I'm not all that hungry, that's why I didn't order much. Are you sure a salad and soup is all you want?"

Marlowe frowned, then blew out a breath.

"Kai, that's nice that you're asking, but I know my own mind. Even if I've probably had the second roughest day of my life, I can figure out what I want for dinner. The soup will feel good after all the stress I went through, and the salad is because I haven't eaten a vegetable in four days, but I'll probably just look at it. However, it'll make me feel better that I at least ordered it." She paused. "So, in the future, would you please not think you know better than I do about what I want?"

She said the last sentence in the sweetest voice imaginable, but she sure as hell got her point across. I couldn't help but grin. "I hear you. I won't do it again. Thanks for speaking up for yourself, I really appreciate knowing where I stand."

She blew out another long breath, and that's when I realized she'd been holding it. I kissed her temple. "Lady, you just keep getting better and better in my eyes."

She looked surprised.

"It's true."

The server came back at that moment so I couldn't follow up on that line of talk. I got the feeling that her relationship with the stalker had really done a number on her in a lot of ways.

When we were done with dinner, I asked Marlowe to wait at the table for five additional minutes while I got things from my room. I came back with my rucksack full.

"What's that for?"

"I'm driving you back to your place and sleeping on the couch."

"Why would you do that?"

Huh?

"Marlowe, somebody tried to kill you today. Of course I'm sleeping on your couch. Or you could sleep here in my room. But there's only one bed, and the couch is more like a loveseat. I do want to sleep with you, but I don't think tonight is the night, do you?"

I watched as her brown eyes turned almost black. Her body relaxed even deeper into mine, and her hand that had been resting on the table came up to my chest and started petting me.

"Tonight would be the perfect time for us to make love," she murmured sensually.

With just those words, said with that tone of voice, I got so hard, I could hammer nails.

"Marlowe, I don't want to take advantage of you if you're overwrought."

"What did I just say about you questioning my choices?"

"Oh yeah." I couldn't help but grin. "Well, we better get to your house fast, I'm feeling pretty needy."

"What's wrong with the one bed in your room here?"

She was still using her sexy voice. She needed to stop or I would never be able to walk out of here.

I thought about it. I knew what she'd said about

knowing her own mind, but somebody had tried to kill her today, and her beloved dog had almost died.

Fuck!

Okay, I'd take her up to my room. I'd hold her. *That's the ticket.* She needed to be held. And my damn cock would just have to get with the program.

I slid out of the seat and held out my hand so that I could help her out as well. I slipped on my rucksack so it was balanced evenly, then held her hand as we exited the restaurant. The maître d gave us a smile as we left the restaurant. We were able to go to the elevators without passing reception.

"This is a wonderful room," Marlowe exclaimed. "You have a great view of the forest."

"It is," I agreed. I shed the backpack and went over to where she stood next to the window. She turned around to face me, then stepped closer so that we were touching, chest to breast.

"I like your bed, too. It's king size. Perfect."

"I like it, too," I muttered.

"I'd kiss you, but you're too tall. How about if I do this?" she asked, as she reached up and slipped her arms around my neck. She put just the slightest pressure on my neck, just as she always did. She remembered that I had been injured there. Just one more thing I liked about Marlowe Jones; she remembered things like that and was always aware and considerate.

"If you do that, then I'm going to do this." I grazed my lips over hers, just a soft brush, teasing us both.

Her hands moved up, tangling in my hair, nails scraping my scalp. God, that felt good. I licked her bottom lip, and she opened. This kiss was like nothing I had ever experienced before. Gentle and needy in a way that demanded more. My tongue slowly pushed for entrance, and Marlowe sucked me inside her warmth.

I felt her body sink against me. Such a precious, subtle weight. I felt the hard peaks of her nipples scraping my chest through the layers of our clothes and as our kiss deepened I couldn't help but wonder what the tips of her breasts would look like. Taste like.

Marlowe began to rub her tongue against mine and I was back in the moment, swirling in the sensual tempest that was Marlowe's kiss. She broke away for air, and I took that moment to bite her lower lip. I heard a low growl, and I laughed. I wanted to sweep her up and carry her to my bed, but I couldn't. Instead, I turned and propelled her toward the bed.

"Oh yes," she purred. "I'll get to see you naked."

I closed my eyes for just a moment and realized that for the first time since all of my operations, somebody other than a medical professional was going to see my mangled flesh.

"I hope you like scars," I teased.

"They turn me on more than tattoos." She grinned up at me. "You show me your scars, and I'll show you my tattoo. Deal?"

I laughed. She constantly made me laugh. I loved that.

"You first," I said, as I pushed her to a sitting position on the side of the bed, then knelt down between her legs. Before I could even blink, she had her t-shirt over her head.

She hissed.

"Dammit." I could see where she had been pulled back by the seatbelt. "You need ice on that bruise." I stood up to get the laundry bag out of the closet so I could fill it with ice.

"Don't you dare leave me. I'll ice this after sex."

"You'll ice before sex."

She grabbed my hand with both of hers. "Please, Kai. I need this. It's more than just sex. I'm going to lose it if you don't make love to me. I need this closeness, the feeling of being wanted."

"Baby, you are wanted. And you'll be just as wanted after I put ice on your bruise."

"Just wait for a few minutes," she urged.

I slowly smiled. "If you think this would only take a few minutes, you've been sleeping with the wrong men."

She bit her bottom lip. "Man. I slept with the wrong man."

I got what she was saying. She'd only slept with the dickwad stalker. She was right, she needed this. Ice could wait. She must have seen the decision in my eyes, because she smiled in relief.

"Can you take off your shirt now?"

I nodded, then pulled off my tee.

I waited for her to say something.

"You're more beautiful than I imagined."

I thought she was bullshitting me, until I saw her eyes roam over my chest and abs like I was ice cream on a hot day. I knelt back down and pulled off her shoes and socks, then pulled off her jeans and panties. That left her in just her bra.

"Is it going to hurt if I take off your bra?" I didn't know if it would feel better or worse with the bruising.

"Are you going to touch my breasts if you take off my bra?"

"Definitely."

"Then I'll feel much better if you take it off." The pleasure was evident in her tone.

I reached behind her and unclasped her bra, then slowly lowered the straps and pulled down the cups of her bra until I pulled it off. She sighed.

"It feels better now."

"That's good, Honey."

The hungry look in her eyes would have brought me to my knees if I hadn't already been on them.

"Now you take off the rest of your clothes," she demanded.

"Not yet. I like it just where I am."

"But—"

I didn't let her continue, I just leaned and licked. She tried to close her legs, but I pushed them open even farther.

"Kai," she wailed.

I was getting somewhere.

I parted the lips of her sex and caught a glimpse of heaven. She glistened with desire, and I hadn't even really started. I lapped up her slick essence, and it was the best thing I had ever tasted. Then I used my whiskers to abrade her sensitive flesh and she yelled out my name even louder.

I lifted up. "Do you like that?"

"Yes. God, yes. Again."

I grinned and brushed my chin against her clit. This time when she called my name, it was muffled. I looked up and saw she had her hand over her mouth. I used my thumb to swirl circles around her sensitive flesh. Her whimpers were music to my ears.

I was aching to get inside her, but giving her pleasure was much more important.

"Kai, I'm close." Her words were a strained whisper.

Slowly I inserted a finger inside her. I looked up to see her head shaking side to side.

"Too much," she said. Then she added, "Don't stop."

I found that perfect spot and rubbed it as my thumb continued to circle her clit. Now she was just chanting *don't stop*. I was breaking out in a sweat. I needed to give her this. I needed to watch her come.

I swirled faster, and then inserted a second finger. I could see how close she was. It was beautiful.

"Now, Marlowe. Now."

"Yes," she moaned. "Yes."

She bucked upward. Her channel clamped down on my fingers.

Her cries didn't stop as she twisted back and forth.

I knelt up high and looked at her face. She had never looked more beautiful.

16

Vaguely I watched as Kai stripped off the rest of his clothes. At least it was vague until I saw his cock. It was perfect. It jutted out from the dark hair of his groin, thick and long. The head was almost purple and I could see a little bit of pre-come from the top. He was going to fill me up. I was pretty sure I was going to like this. I hoped I was going to like this.

I watched as he rolled a condom over his erection, then he knelt on the bed beside me and leaned in for a kiss. Whatever bit of trepidation I'd been feeling flew out of my mind.

God, could he kiss.

At first he was gentle, with light brushes that tantalized, but soon it morphed into frustrating teases. I grasped his cheeks and lifted my head so I could smash my lips against his. I licked across his lips, and he opened his mouth and then closed his lips around my tongue. It felt so good. When his tongue started to stroke mine, I lost my mind.

I don't know when he'd moved, but now he straddled me without ever breaking our kiss. His hands were braced on either side of my head and his chest hair was now grazing against the tips of my breasts. So much sensation. I was caught in a whirlwind.

He lifted his head, breaking the kiss finally, and I whimpered. I wanted the kiss to go on forever, but as I saw his eyes look downward to my breasts, I moaned when I realized everything else he was about to do to me.

"Damn, look at you. You're so pretty and pink."

He rolled to his side and propped himself up on his elbow. Then his other hand cupped my breast, his thumb lashing my nipple, back and forth, back and forth. He was driving me crazy. He bent over me, and I was sure he was going to take my nipple into his mouth. Instead he placed soft kisses all along my bruises.

"It scares the fuck out of me that you could have been killed today. You're going to have to tell me what happened. You know that, right?"

"Later," I gasped. His kisses moved back up, closer to my aching flesh. All the time he had been kissing my bruise, he had been brushing his thumb over my nipple. I knew those little cries were coming from my mouth, and even though I tried to stop them, I couldn't.

Then he was there, at my nipple.

Licking,

Laving.

Sucking.

I was going out of my mind.

"You taste so good."

I looked at him, his expression intent at what he was doing.

"I want to feel you against me," I pleaded.

"Some other time, not when you're banged up like you are." He moved upwards and I was soon drowning in the pleasure of his kiss. Long, slow, sensuous minutes, we communicated with kisses. It was the most beautiful thing I had ever experienced, but I still wanted more. I moved my hand downward and gripped his condom-covered cock, then squeezed.

Kai groaned. Just one more thing I would savor from our time together.

I widened my legs. "Please Kai, I need you inside me."

"I don't want to hurt you. Are you good to be on top?"

I moved to roll over, then winced.

"That answers that. It's okay, I've got you covered." He knelt up between my legs and pulled me towards him. Soon my thighs were draped over his, and I saw his beautiful erection close to my core. I closed my eyes and sighed. It was everything I wanted.

"Open your eyes, Sweetheart."

I did, and I looked up into his face. He was looking down, concentrating on the most important task in the world.

"Kai?"

His head jerked upward and he smiled at me.

"Are you ready?" His voice came out in a rasp.

"More than."

I felt him begin to press in and I shuddered. I saw the question in his eyes.

"Keep going," I whispered.

He pushed further, and I held in my gasp, but good Lord. He was a lot to take in.

His gaze flicked between my eyes, to where we were connected, and back up to my eyes. I continued to smile as I felt his penetration. When he was finally seated, I let out a long breath. I reached up and stroked his rippling abdomen. It was clear that he was trying to hold himself under control. Poor man needed some prompting.

"Please, Kai," I whispered.

"Give me a moment, sweetheart." He huffed out the words.

"No. I need you now."

He must have seen something in my eyes, because he began to move. He pulled slowly out, then pushed back in. Again, and then again. It became a sensual dance as he pulled and pushed and I moved up and back, but with every sweet motion, I felt my orgasm coming closer. I wasn't going to last, but I didn't want to go without Kai.

He dipped forward, slamming one hand to the side of my head, and then his lips met mine for a ferocious kiss. We were both mad with want and need. I shoved up again, and he thrust harder. I loved every second.

He moved his mouth to my ear.

"Now," he commanded.

"No. Not without you."

"You're going to be the death of me, Marlowe."

I dug my heels into his ass and felt his entire body shudder as he thrust deep. He catapulted me into a world of ecstasy I never could have imagined. I was lost, and I loved it.

"You promise me you'll keep this icepack on all day, okay?"

"Boy, you're bossy. Were you in a command position in the Army?"

I gave her a half smile. "I commanded men sometimes. Now will you keep the icepack on?"

"I would be stupid not to. After all, that's what the doctor said to do, too."

"And we're in agreement that I'm cooking dinner tonight, right?" I reiterated for the third time.

"Yes, oh exalted one. You're cooking. I'm icing and resting. I've got it."

"And if you go to the animal hospital, I'll know about it, and I won't be happy. I've already taken you there twice. Once before the visit to Doc Evans, and once after."

Her bottom lip jutted out like a little girl. It was adorable.

"I promise. And anyway, how was I going to go do it, since I don't have my 4Runner?"

"You're smart. You would have figured out a way."

"Seriously, Kai, I'm not stupid. I'm going to stay here in *Randy's* room," she put air quotes around the name Randy, "and order room service. I won't go out. I'll wait for you to come back so we can go back to my house."

I bent over and rubbed my nose against hers. "Thank you. That makes me very happy."

"Now go do whatever manly thing you have to do this morning, and come back soon. I'm sure I'll be sick of TV and your magazines by three o'clock."

I smiled at her, then left the hotel room. I hoped like hell there was going to be a guest at the reception desk so I could get by Roberta without an inquisition.

"Hey Doll!"

I winced. No such luck.

"Hi Ro. In a hurry. Gotta go."

"Not so fast. I need to know if I should tell the restaurant if our new visitor is going to want lunch. The restaurant likes it if they have a heads-up."

I sighed. I was ninety-nine percent sure what she was saying was bullshit, but on the one percent chance that she was telling the truth, I went over to her.

"Lacy told me about Marlowe's near miss yesterday. Is she alright?"

"Who's Lacy?"

"She's the dispatcher and all around go-to girl at the Sheriff's office."

I frowned. "She shouldn't be telling you that kind of information."

"Oh, don't worry Doll, it's okay. She's my cousin, once removed. She knows it's safe with me. Anyway, this isn't nearly as bad as when Millie, Lisa and little Bella were held hostage. Now that had everyone talking."

I shook my head.

Really?

"Yes, Marlowe might order lunch," I admitted. "Can you do me a favor?"

"Sure thing."

"The safety belt she was wearing did a number on her torso. She needs to be icing every twenty minutes. Can you check in on her?"

"Absolutely. Wanted to size her up, anyway. My Forrest is going to be in her class this year. Wanted to make sure she had the fire to put him in his place when necessary."

"I don't think that's going to be a problem." I grinned. I thought about the way she politely told me off at the restaurant. "She can definitely put Forrest in his place if need be."

"That's what I wanted to hear." Roberta smiled with satisfaction. "But I'll be checking in on her. When are you going to be back?"

"About fourteen hundred hours."

"Say what?"

"About two o'clock."

"Gotcha."

I pulled Simon's card out of my wallet and headed out the door. I had my phone to my ear by the time I reached my truck.

"Onyx Security," a woman answered.

So, Simon's company had a name.

"Can I speak to Simon Clark?"

"May I ask who's calling?"

"Kai Davies."

"One moment, please."

I had my truck running and my phone connected to Bluetooth by the time Simon got onto the line.

"Hello, Kai. I was expecting your call. Did you have a chance to look over Nash's report?"

"There wasn't much to it."

"You didn't see what he sent over an hour ago?"

I pulled out to Hwy 321. "Nope. What was in it?"

"The entire file on Denny Rasmussen, and it wasn't pretty. We're talking things like letters with pictures of her going to work, going home. He had pictures of her in her classroom. Harris determined those were taken about thirty feet away from the school, so he was inside the school's property. Then there was the woman's finger he sent to her, with a fake diamond ring on it. He asked her to marry him in that package."

"He killed a woman?" I shouted.

"According to the police, this finger had been frozen and immersed in formaldehyde. It was taken from a corpse."

"So why wasn't he arrested?" I shouted again.

"Couldn't prove any of this was him. When the finger showed up on her doorstep, he was out of town on a business trip, plenty of witnesses."

"So what! He had someone else deliver it."

"There was nothing definitive to prove it was him, but Harris believed it was Rasmussen, so he got the order of protection. He had her re-up it every year when it expired."

"And that stopped the guy?"

"Not according to Harris. About the time the restraining order went into effect, he started dating someone new. But she broke up with him three months ago."

I slammed my hand against my steering wheel so hard that it hurt. "Fuck!"

"That's what I said."

"And the principal?"

"She's small potatoes. However, there is some-thing interesting. There is a state senator who is pushing the principal to settle the suit."

"What does he have to do with Marlowe's wrongful termination? Is he a friend of Marlowe's?"

"Don't know. Need to ask."

"I will this afternoon."

"What the hell, Kai? I thought you were going to stay with her." Simon sounded pissed.

"I didn't leave her at her house. I left her at the Whispering Pines. Nobody will know she's there."

"Hell, Kai, half the town knows you're dating. If she's not at her house, the next logical place to look will be at your hotel room."

"I'm not an idiot. I got her a different room than mine. It's under the name Randy Dickerson."

Simon laughed. "Were you channeling a thirteen-year-old boy when you came up with that name?"

I sighed. "It was the first fake name that popped into my head. Give me a break."

"And here I wanted to talk to you about a job. If that's the best you can come up with, now I'm not so sure."

"I told you, I'm only passing through."

"Seems to me you have a girlfriend who is staying permanently, and you're doing physical therapy on someone that is going to need it for at least six months according to Doc Evans."

"Can it, Simon."

"Have you talked to your brother yet?"

"I should be today."

"Good luck, Kai. Gotta go."

"Good-bye."

I ended the call, and continued up the pathetic excuse of a road up to Bernie's house. Why they hadn't told me about it in the first place, I didn't know.

17

Bernie had said there wasn't time to dick around with Beau calling a different number. So I was just supposed to go up to Bernie's house again, which frustrated me to no end. I didn't want to leave Marlowe alone. I knew she'd be safe at the hotel under a different name. Yes, Jasper Creek talked, but people knew enough to keep their mouths shut when it was important. I just didn't want to leave her while she was still worried about Chaos. And especially after we'd made love. I didn't know where this was going between us, and what we had seemed more fragile than ever.

As for the ATV I'd been driving, Dave the guy who owned the hardware store had driven it back to Bernie's place. As I made it up the rough road, my hands began to sweat.

What the hell?

It had been at least thirteen years since I had been

this nervous. It had been my first mission, but as soon as I was in the thick of things, my training had kicked in and I did what I needed to do. But how in the hell do you train for meeting a twin brother that you never knew you had?

I pulled up next to Bernie's A-frame and parked my truck. He was waiting for me on his deck. He was holding two beers. Okay, apparently Bernie thought the way to handle meeting your twin for the first time included alcohol before noon. I was up for it.

I climbed up the stairs.

"Where's Mora?" I asked.

"She's in town visiting with Trenda, Maddie and Evie."

"Would Evie be the woman who owns part of Whispering Pines?" I grabbed the offered beer.

"Yep. She, Aiden, and their boys show up about twice a year, and she comes out a bit more."

I considered making more conversation, but I couldn't. "When is Beau supposed to call?"

"He'll call between twelve-thirty and one." He popped his phone off his belt and threw it at me and I caught it. Checking the time, I had twenty minutes to kill.

Might as well ask more about the town.

"How'd you end up here?"

Bernie settled into a chair. "I was working for a big corporation. When a relative of mine died and left me this land, I asked for my retirement package early and built this house. I was sick of the rat race, and sick of living on top of my neighbors."

"Well, there's no chance of that here." He smiled and toasted me before he took his first sip of beer. "You seem pretty plugged in for someone who doesn't live in town."

"I go get my coffee from the Jolt and sit there for a while. Almost everyone goes in there in the mornings. Grab breakfast at Down Home and my groceries from Rogers. Do that about twice a week. Once a week I go to the retirement home to visit Luther and Violet Randolph. They lived up on the mountain most of their lives, but with Luther's Alzheimer's, they had to move to town."

"I've missed the Jolt."

"Java Jolt. It's run by Ruby Garner. It's a block off the town square. I didn't think she'd be able to make a go of it, but that girl has grit. Her pastries outdo Pearl's and Down Home's, but don't tell them I said so, otherwise I won't be allowed back into their restaurants."

I chuckled. *Truth.* "Besides Marlowe and me, what other news do you have to share?"

"Everybody is on the lookout for a big black truck. Nobody likes the idea of somebody trying to run our teacher off the road."

That did my heart good to hear, and reassured me that no one was going to talk to a stranger looking for Marlowe. It didn't ease my nervousness about talking to Beau. *My twin.* I glanced at the time. Five, maybe ten minutes, and the phone in my hand would ring, my brother on the other end.

"And everybody's worried about Chloe Avery," Bernie went on. "Oops, I mean Post. We haven't seen hide nor hair of her since her last miscarriage. Her sisters go to her house, but she hasn't gone over to theirs. Not even when Evie brings her boys to town. Of course, that might be rubbing salt into a wound."

"Bernie, I think you're oversharing now."

He took a swallow of his beer. "You're right, I might be. It's just that the whole town is worried. Not just about her, we're worried about her husband Zarek. He's one of our fire fighters."

I gave him a pointed glance.

"Got you. There's a Town Hall meeting coming up and the agenda has some juicy items on it. We're going to be discussing—"

The phone rang.

Bernie jutted his chin at the phone. "Better answer it. That's Beau's ring tone. I'm going to go into the house."

Bernie hightailed it inside while I let it ring one more time, palms clammy as I wiped them on my pants, then pressed answer on the FaceTime call.

"Hello."

For a split second, I thought the phone's camera was on the selfie setting. Looking at Beau was like looking into a mirror. Only I was looking at a really tired and pissed off version of myself.

"Bernie—" Beau started. Then he stopped, mouth open and eyes wide. "B-Brady?"

"Retired, Warrant Officer, Delta Force, Kai Davies, at your service."

He quickly closed his mouth and squinted his eyes. "*Kai?* What the...? Who?" Beau took in a deep breath. "What the fuck, Brady? Where in the hell have you been?" Beau practically shouted. "You being gone killed our mother, do you know that?"

That was one hell of a hard blow.

"Beau, I didn't know about you. Swear to God, I didn't know about you."

"You're there. In Jasper Creek. You must have known something. Where were you all this time?"

"Alaska. Ronald said I was an only child born in Dillingham. According to him, my mother ran off when I was a baby because she was a hussy."

Beau flinched at that like I'd just punched him.

"I didn't know the truth."

"Who the hell is Ronald?"

"Our father. He called himself Ronald." I shook my head, frustrated. This wasn't what I expected and it wasn't going well. I tried again. "I found a photo of the two of us as little kids. It said Brady and Grady, Jasper Creek. Found it three years ago, but I was still active. After the injury and my retirement, decided to follow-up. Discover the truth. You're Grady, and I guess that makes me Brady."

Beau took a deep breath. "How'd you end up at Bernie's?"

I found a picture of my father in an old newspaper photo, only he was Arthur." I shook my head. "*Our* father. Bernie had your number, so…" I shrugged. "You complete your mission, or is this just a break?"

He squinted at me again. "What mission?"

Of course he'd deny being on a mission.

"I'm Delta Force, remember?"

He nodded. "Mission completed." He took a deep breath as he just stared at me. "Hmm. I guess when Bernie texted on WhatsApp that I should brace for this FaceTime call, he wasn't kidding."

"Guess not."

"You said you retired. Medical discharge?"

I only nodded.

"What injury?"

"Shrapnel in the neck, above the Kevlar. Multiple surgeries. They didn't think I would walk again. Proved them wrong, but the only job I'd get was pushing paper."

Beau snorted. "Yeah, that wouldn't be any good."

"Got that right."

"Was he violent?"

His abrupt subject change caught me off-guard and it took me a second to understand. "Dad?"

Beau nodded. I saw him swallow. Hard.

"Sometimes," I admitted. "Can you tell me about Mom?"

I watched and heard Beau sigh. "It's a long story."

"When's your next leave?"

"I've got plans."

I chuckled. "Yeah, Little Grandma told me you were jumping off bases."

Beau snorted. "I loved that old lady. Good to hear she's still kicking."

"So, you're coming back? Checking things out?" I couldn't keep the hope out of my voice, but fuck it, if he didn't come here, I'd go to him.

But seriously, Brady. *Kai.*" He looked at me and clenched his jaw. Was he seeing me or the man who broke his mother's heart? I couldn't be sure. "Jasper Creek is not my favorite place."

This time I sighed. "I hear you. Still, I would like to hear more about Mom."

"I get it, brother." He stared at me for a long time while I let the fact that he called me brother sink in. It felt good.

"I'll see what I can do," he finally answered.

"I'd appreciate it," I said around the huge lump in my throat.

Beau lifted his chin. "In the meantime, I'd like to set up a call when I have more time. I've got to go in for a debrief."

Didn't that sound familiar?

He didn't say anything more, just stared at me again. It was seriously like looking in a mirror. Then the left side of his mouth tilted up and a dimple popped. A dimple I didn't have.

I remember that!

"Shit, Brady, I'm blown away, but so damned excited. I hope you know that."

"Same." I swallowed around an even bigger lump. Choking back tears.

"Retirement's made you soft," Beau chuckled.

I laughed. "Fuck you."

"Right back at you." He paused, flashed that dimple again, then said, "Bye, Brother."

The screen went black.

Driving back from Bernie's I was anxious to talk to someone about Beau. I would have thought it would've been Clay, but actually it was Marlowe. It made me stop and think about just how close we'd gotten in the last month.

Damn, how did that happen?

I just waved to Gretchen when I flew through reception at the Whispering Pines Inn. The elevator was taking too long, so I took the stairs. When I got inside the room, I wasn't surprised to find Marlowe practically crawling out of her skin.

"Did you talk to him?"

"I did."

"You don't sound excited about it."

"Let's talk about it over dinner. The sign downstairs said the special was salmon."

"Nothing personal, but I'm never all that

impressed with an ocean fish in a land-locked state. Now if they had said trout or catfish…"

"So you're basically a snob. Good to find this out early in the relationship." I sat down on the couch beside her and pulled her carefully into my arms.

"You know I'm not fine china. I can handle it if you hold me closer."

"Let's save that for next week, shall we?"

Marlowe let out a long breath.

"What was that for?"

"I was afraid that after talking to Beau you might be thinking about leaving town."

She had her face nestled in my neck so I couldn't see her expression. I needed to, so I pushed her back and tilted her chin up.

"Sweetheart. I don't plan to leave anytime soon."

"That's not what you've been saying. What's more, you're living in a hotel. Two signs that you're not planning on staying."

"Let me tell you about my conversation with Beau, hmm?"

She looked at me with those deep brown eyes and nodded.

"He kind of reminded me of me."

She snorted. "He is your twin."

"Smartass. Let me finish."

"He's in special operations, too."

"I looked that up. That's a lot more specialized than just being in the Army or Marines or Navy. You have to be a lot more trained, and you go into more hazardous situations. The death toll is higher too."

"Not by much. Because we're so well trained, we can take out the enemy and take care of ourselves."

"Is that how you ended up in hospitals for almost a year?" Her voice was husky. It was obvious that she cared and was scared.

"First off, I'm not going back to the teams, so that's something you don't have to worry about, and second of all, my injury was the first major one that our team sustained in the six years since we've been together. Marlowe, you need to take my word, we're good."

Her fingers bit into my biceps as she tried to read the truth in my eyes. She finally nodded her head. "So do you think Beau is good, too?"

"I would bet my last dollar that he is."

"Did you talk about it? What you did. The special operations stuff."

"Honey, we don't talk about that stuff. Our missions are secret. We don't talk to anybody but our team members about what we do." I paused. *I might as well ask the question.* "Is that something you could handle?"

She frowned. "Why not? If that's the way it had to be, of course I could. It's the same way as when I'm dealing with a troubled kid. If I have to take him or her to counseling, I wouldn't tell you about it."

I leaned in for a kiss. "You're just about perfect, Ms. Jones."

"Tell me what I need to do to get to a ten. I want a perfect score."

"We'll discuss that in the bedroom."

18

I woke up and Kai's side of the bed was cold. I wasn't surprised; it was that way yesterday morning, too. Mr. Muscles was out exercising, which I totally applauded considering the body it created.

However, it sucked that it was so early and I couldn't call Sue and tell her everything that was going on with Kai. I know I should have felt bad for her that she had dental surgery yesterday and couldn't talk, but I felt more bad for me that I couldn't tell her everything. I was totally a bad friend. I picked up my phone and decided to text. She had her phone on do-not-disturb until seven in the morning, so it wouldn't hurt that I was texting her at five forty-five.

Sue - A good friend wouldn't have had dental surgery the day somebody tried to kill me and I had spectacular sex with an Army Special Operator with lots and lots and lots of muscles and a really, really, really big muscle. We're through. – Signed your friend Marlowe.

That should garner me a call.

I hopped out of bed and got into the shower. I liked the bath shower gel that they had here better than the stuff that I used. I was so buying some from their gift shop before we checked out. I stopped mid-scrub. I still had no idea as to what Kai's plans were for the future. He said he wasn't planning on leaving anytime soon, and he wanted to know if I could handle the life of a special operator. But what did that matter, it's not like he was going to be one of those anymore. I started in with my loofah again. At this rate I wouldn't have any skin left.

I really needed to go with the flow, except that wasn't really my personality. I liked to control things if I could; of course, if I couldn't, then oh well. Kind of. Like Denny. He was a monster that required counseling. I didn't foresee anything about Kai forcing me into counseling. Long talks with Sue? Yes. Counseling, no.

By the time I was out of the shower and had my hair blown dry, I'd received two phone calls and three messages from Sue. I looked at my watch.

Perfect. We should have at least forty-five minutes before Kai gets back.

"I'll take the Colt 45, the AK-47, and the Glock 17."

The gray-bearded gentleman working behind the counter looked me up and down. "How long were you in the service, son?"

"Didn't make it to my fifteen. Injury."

He nodded.

"You need this much firepower?"

"I sincerely hope not, but I believe in being safe rather than sorry."

"Ain't that the truth." He lisped from the tobacco in his mouth.

"Can you go to the law?"

"I'm down in Jasper Creek. Good sheriff there, name's Nash Rivers. He's on it. But this is my woman. Like I said, I just want to keep her safe."

He nodded slowly. "Sound thinking. Let me get you loaded up with ammo."

I watched as he took out box after box after box. I grinned.

"I'll ring you up over here."

"Thank you, sir."

"Keep her safe, that's all the thanks I need."

I went out to my truck. I'd already had a toolbox installed in the bed of the truck, so I dumped most of my purchases in there, but kept out the Glock and four magazines. It was overkill, but again, I hated the idea of being sorry.

Now I felt good about taking Marlowe back to the house.

"Darn," Marlowe said with a pout.

"What, Sweetheart?"

"I figured with you gone that long, you would have really built up a sweat. Sweat is right on up there with scars."

I laughed. "Sorry, I had some things to take care of in Knoxville."

"What things?"

"I wanted to make sure I had a gun in case somebody decided to pay us a visit when we stayed at your place."

"Well, I have a gun. You should have asked."

I frowned. I wasn't expecting that. Not a schoolteacher.

"Don't give me that look. My dad was in the Navy, remember? He taught me and my sister how to shoot. He thought having a gun was a smart thing for a woman on her own. I agree. And before you ask, yes, I know how to use it, and I used to go to the gun range on a regular basis, I just haven't found one around here."

"What kind is it?"

"Sig Sauer P365."

"Not bad. We'll go out to the range next week. After your bruise heals."

"Yeah, I can think of better things for us to be doing in the meantime."

"Let me guess, visiting Chaos."

She sucked in her lower lip, and I smiled.

"At the moment, that is number one on my list, but just by a smidgeon. Normally making love with you would be number one."

"Glad to hear it was a close call."

"Speaking of calls, I talked to Kizzie. She said that Chaos isn't eating well. I want to stop by my house before going over to the vet's and get Chaos her food. Can we do that?"

"Sure."

"Thanks." She stepped up and kissed my jaw, but I wasn't letting her get away with that. No way. I pulled her into my arms and gave her the kiss I'd been dreaming about all morning long. Marlowe caught fire in my arms, and I was in heaven.

"When you said get her food, you know I just thought you were getting some cans of special dog food, don't you?"

"Yeah." I poured some of the pumpkin puree into the mixture of ground chicken, fish oil, steamed vegetables, and rice. Kai came into the kitchen and put his chin on my shoulder.

"Do you cook all the meals you make with this kind of precision?"

"For just me? No. For someone else? Definitely."

"How much longer is this going to take?"

"We're close to the end," I promised him. When it was almost done, I added a quarter of a teaspoon of cinnamon and a tablespoon of sugar.

"What in the hell did you just put in there?" Kai demanded to know.

"Chaos loves pumpkin pie. I give her a slice every once in a while. That's why I chose this recipe, because it calls for pumpkin puree. So I add a little cinnamon and sugar, just so she has a little bit more of a taste of pie."

"You are such a softie," Kai said as he nuzzled my ear.

Thank God the boiling water part of the process was done already.

"So will you make me special treats when I'm sick?" he asked me.

My heart jolted. The very idea of him being around when he was sick made me joyous. "I don't know, what kind of patient are you? Are you the stubborn kind who won't do as they're told? Petulant? Whiny?"

"All of the above," he whispered. His breath blew across my neck, giving me goosebumps.

"Then of course I will fix you special treats," I promised. "I'll also put a cold compress on your warm brow, and force you to wear an ice pack."

He didn't laugh. Instead, his teeth grazed the side of my neck. I looked down in the bowl. Chaos' food was done. I turned around and put my arms around Kai's shoulders and lifted my head up for a kiss.

Kai's head shot up at the sound of the doorbell.

What the hell?

I'd lived here for seven weeks and hardly anybody had come to my house. Why now?

"Stay in the kitchen, Marlowe. Let me see who it is."

I was shocked to see a gun in his hand.

"Kai, somebody out to kill me isn't going to knock on the door," I protested.

"You can never be too careful. Stay where you are, Sweetheart, yeah?"

"Yeah."

I heard Kai answer the door, and there was some conversation. I heard my name mentioned a few times, and I really wanted to go out there, but I didn't. I'd promised Kai. The deal was, when you made a promise, you kept it. Full stop.

I heard him before I saw him. Kai came storming around the corner.

"Marlowe, this isn't a big deal, okay?" He had both hands on either side of my neck. He was looking down at me, his eyes were the color of ice.

That meant something was a big deal. A huge deal.

"What?"

"I need you to come out here. Someone wants to give you a letter. That's all. Just take the letter and he'll leave." I could tell he was trying to contain his anger. It felt like anger on my behalf.

"What's the letter about?"

"Just take the letter, and let's get him the hell out of here, and then we can talk about it. Okay?"

I tried to think of what this was about, but Kai was on my side, so I just nodded.

"Okay," I nodded. "Let's go get this over with."

When we got to the door, I saw it was shut. "Where is he?"

"I left him outside."

"Of course you did. Why don't you open the door?"

Kai scowled, then opened the door. "Here she is."

"Are you Marlowe Jones?" the skinny young man asked.

I nodded.

"Do you have ID?"

"She's not getting ID for you. This is the address, she's the occupant. Give her the letter," Kai growled.

The man backed up a step, looked at me, and held out his trembling hand with a letter. "This is for you, ma'am. You've been served."

He looked over at Kai, then dashed down the steps to an old Chevy Nova and drove away as fast as he could.

I felt my heart race. Dammit, this had to be about my lawsuit with Principal Sykes.

"Come on inside, Marlowe. Let's get you some

wine, or tea, or coffee, or something and you can open the letter. Then we can go visit Chaos."

I started breathing again at the idea of visiting Chaos. But then I felt the paper in my hands. Seriously, what now?

Kai ushered me back into the kitchen. "What is the lady's pleasure?"

"Just iced tea. Plenty of sugar."

"Coming right up."

I ripped open the letter and started reading. The more I read, the more it didn't make any sense. Kai set the iced tea on the counter beside me.

"Can you read this?" I held out the letter to him.

"Sure."

I sipped my tea as he read.

"This is weird. This house is obviously Beau's. Who else could it be from?" Kai asked.

"It says I have twenty-four hours to vacate the premises."

"Fuck that shit. You're going to stay where you are. There isn't a chance in hell that Beau's evicting you. I just talked to him yesterday."

Kai turned the envelope over and squinted at the return address. "I think we should call this attorney and see what's going on."

19

The lawyer's address was a post office box in Gatlinburg. He had a website and a chatbox, but no phone number.

Great.

"I can't believe that Principal Sykes would go to these kind of lengths to get me to stop the suit. I've got to call Sue. I mean, is her job on the line or something?"

I looked at Kai who was still looking at the letter, while I was holding my tablet and trying to google any information I could find on this lawyer or any dirt I could dig up on Loretta Sykes.

"I'm not sure this is related to the guys who ran you off the road," Kai said quietly.

"What do you mean?"

"Why would someone go from trying to kill you, then go to trying to harass you? That makes no sense."

He was right.

"Then who is doing this to me?"

"Maybe this isn't about you. Maybe it's about the house. Maybe somebody's out to steal it from under Beau, because they know he hasn't lived here for so long."

"Only people here in Jasper Creek would know that. I can't imagine somebody from here trying to do that, can you?"

Kai shook his head. "I say it's time to call the sheriff. This whole thing stinks to high heaven."

"I'm not leaving here until Beau tells me to," I told Kai.

"Thatta girl."

He wrapped one arm around my neck and pulled me in for a kiss. Suddenly I could care less if we went to visit the sheriff.

"I had Lacy call the county courthouse," Nash said. I could see by the look on his face, I wasn't going to like what he was going to say next. "This is legal. According to what's on file, someone provided the deed to the house, and it was in their name. They made it clear that they did not give permission for anybody but himself to be living there."

"Do I even have to ask who *he* was?" I was getting a bad feeling.

"Arthur Beaumont," Nash said reluctantly.

"And where is Arthur Beaumont?" I asked as my blood pressure skyrocketed.

"Now Kai, we need to handle this by the book. You know and I know that this can't be legal. That asshole ran out of here almost thirty years ago. He left your Mama to pay on that mortgage. There is no way that house is his." Nash's soothing voice grated like sandpaper.

"Where is my father?" I asked for the second time. Nash must have realized I wasn't fucking around.

"We don't know. Per the county clerk, the only time they can get ahold of the attorney is when he has a court appearance, otherwise he's in the wind."

"That can't be right," Marlowe said. "He has to get new clients some way. And if the judge really needs to get ahold of him, he'd have to be available. The county clerk is wrong."

Marlowe was making sense.

"You're right, but so far, she's the only one I've talked to," Nash admitted. "Look, I've got two guys out with the flu for the third day in a row. I'm swamped.

"I've got you," I said. I plucked the letter out of Nash's hands. "We'll work this out."

"What are you going to do, Kai?" he asked.

"We'll keep you informed."

As soon as we stepped out onto the sidewalk, I could see that Marlowe was antsy. "What is it, Sweetheart?" I asked.

"I really need to get this food to Chaos, and I'd really like to spend some time with her."

I realized the antsyness was probably rooted in anxiety over the house, and nothing soothed Marlowe's anxiety like spending time with Chaos. "Okay, let me drop you off."

"Where are you going?" she asked as she climbed into my truck.

"I'm going to check in with a new friend," I said as I started the engine. "I'll let you know if anything pans out."

Onyx Security wasn't in the middle of town like the rest of the businesses. Somebody must have decided that Jasper Creek and Gatlinburg needed office space between the two cities and built some back in the early 2000s, then came the crash and they were stuck with unrentable space. Simon was probably their first tenant.

When I pulled up I saw that there was only one small sign on one of the doors, and it read Onyx Security. I let myself in. An older woman was manning the desk. She looked all-business.

"Can I help you?"

"I'm wondering if Simon Clark is available. My name is Kai Davies."

"He's working on a hot project at the moment, but I'll see if he has time to see you." She stood up and went down a hallway. Something told me that's what she always said to anybody who didn't have an appointment. Two minutes later she reappeared.

"They can see you now."

"They?"

"Simon Clark and Roan Thatcher. They head up Onyx Security," she said proudly.

I wondered if that meant they were the only two employees besides her. When she ushered me down the hall, I was happy to see they weren't living in the lap of luxury. That meant they were saving their pennies on important stuff, like guns, ammunition and surveillance equipment.

I sat down in the small office. Simon gave me a nod and the other man smiled at me.

Simon looked irritated. "I told you I'd give you anything as soon as I had it. I don't have anything yet."

"I've got something new."

Suddenly Simon didn't look nearly as irritated.

"Don't mind him, he hasn't had his fourth cup of coffee today." The man seated across from Simon stood up. "I'm Roan Thatcher. I work with this grumpy old man. It's nice to meet you, Kai. What branch of the service did you work in?"

"Army."

Roan didn't say anything. He crossed his arms and waited.

"Delta," I finally muttered.

"Was that really so hard?" Roan asked.

"Since we're in the share circle, what units did you work in?"

"I was a Navy SEAL Commander," Simon admitted.

"Marine Raider," Roan said proudly.

I filed that little nugget away. It would be interesting to know if he and my brother ever served together.

"So what do you have for us?" Simon asked. He was not a patient man.

I threw the letter on his desk. "That."

Simon took the letter out of the envelope and quickly scanned it, then passed it over to Roan who did the same thing. Simon was now looking at the envelope. He looked up at me.

"What have you found out so far?"

"According to Nash, it's legit. He said it's been processed through the Sevier County courthouse. His contact is a clerk by the name of Lacy. He's had two guys out with the flu for three days and he doesn't have the manpower to check this out. Marlowe and I have gotten only so far. I want to hire you."

"You've found out more than that, haven't you?" Simon wanted to know.

"I found out the attorney on the return address has a website, but only has that PO box. He doesn't have a phone number, only a chatbox on his site."

"The court has to have a way to get ahold of him," Roan pointed out.

I held back a sarcastic response. "Agreed."

Simon tapped the envelope. "We'll take it from here."

"I haven't gotten to the good part yet."

Simon raised his eyebrows.

"According to the county clerk, a guy by the name of Arthur Beaumont said that he has the deed to the house, and he hasn't authorized anybody to be living at his residence. That's the reason he filed for an Unconditional Quit Notice."

"Fuck. Is that who I think it is?" Roan asked.

"Yep, that would be my dad. Or my dad's original name, Arthur Beaumont. I don't know how he has the deed to the house, but he just up and left my mother and Grady almost thirty years ago. He hasn't paid a dime on that house. How in the hell he figures he owns that house, is beyond me. Not only do I want that attorney found, I want my fucking father found. And when you know where he is, I want in on the takedown. Are we clear?"

By that time I was looking straight at Simon.

"Crystal clear. I don't blame you one damn bit. I'm sure we'll find your dad through the attorney. Give us a day."

I nodded and got up from my seat. "This is still second priority. First priority is Marlowe's welfare. Let me know if you find out anything about who is behind running her off the road."

"We need to talk to her about the state senator," Roan said.

"I'm on it," I bit out. "She doesn't need to talk to anyone else today. She's over at the vet, making sure her dog is okay."

"Understood." Simon stood up and leaned across his desk to shake my hand. Roan held out his hand as well.

"Expect to hear from us no later than tomorrow," Simon called out as I was leaving his office.

"I'll hold you to it."

20

___

When I left Onyx, I texted Marlowe to see if she was ready for me to pick her up. She said she wasn't, which really didn't come as that big of a surprise. She and the vet were probably exchanging recipes. Since I had a little bit of time on my hands I decided to track down Java Jolt. It was easy enough when I got to the town square, since there was a sign on the side of the hardware store pointing back a block to the coffee shop.

Bells jingled when I opened the door and the scent of coffee came at me like a heavenly wind. There were three women in line before me. I realized they were all together and one woman was paying. Good, I would get to the counter faster. When I did, I asked for a black cup of coffee, and any pastry she would recommend. She had smiled at me when I first walked up, but when I suggested she choose the pastry, she gave me a full-watt smile, and she was dazzling. Not as gorgeous as Marlowe, but close.

"Are you Ruby Garner?" I asked.

"Yep." She looked me up and down, then asked. "Are you Kai Davies?"

"How'd you know that?"

"Word gets around." She grinned. "But from what I hear from Pearl, you like all kinds of desserts, so I'm thinking it's going to be hard to go wrong."

"I do have my favorites."

"Would they know how to do algebra?" Her eyes gleamed as she asked that question. She put down the large coffee on the counter, then bent toward the bakery items.

I chuckled. "I think Marlowe even knows calculus," I bragged.

Ruby laughed too as she brought out a cherry turnover and put it on a plate. She pointed to my backpack. "Are you planning on working this morning?"

"I want to make a couple of phone calls and do a little research."

"It's hot out, so go over near the fireplace. There's no fire, but still, in the summer people tend to avoid it. Also, there's a plug if you need it."

I swiped my card to pay for my items and took her advice and headed toward the fireplace. As soon as I was settled, I pulled my laptop out of my backpack. Marlowe had teased me about it. She said I needed to venture into the new decade and get myself a tablet, but I refused to trade-up on anything that wasn't broken. Unless, of course, it was a bigger screen TV.

I took a sip of Ruby's coffee and wondered if she sold bags of it that I could buy as I booted up my laptop. Granted, Simon and Roan looked like they had a handle on shit, especially when it came to Marlowe's old boyfriend and principal, but I really didn't want to sit around with my thumb up my ass and wait for their phone call. Especially when it came to my fucking father.

As usual, my laptop made its normal grinding sounds as it started up, another thing that told Marlowe that I needed to upgrade, or at least back it up. I pretended not to know what backing it up meant just to fuck with her. That had been fun. I took a bite of my cherry turnover and dialed Lucky's number. He was going to be out on a boat, but he was a good guy; he'd take my call if he could.

"Where have you been, you asshole? You almost die and then don't keep us up to date, what the fuck is wrong with you?"

"I'm sorry, did you send some flowers that I should have thanked you for?"

God, I loved this guy.

"We sent a stripper telegram, didn't she show up?"

"You're too cheap to have sent that. Now if Shil had told me that lie, I might have believed it."

"Answer the goddamned question. Where have you been?"

"Calm your ass down. I called you when I was in Walter Reed. I told you they had me up and walking."

"What you told me, and I'll give you an exact quote, was; I can now drag my legs from one end of the parallel bars to the other without falling, end quote. Jesus, Kai, all of us texted you and left you messages. Did it ever occur to you to call or text us back?"

I pinched the bridge of my nose. "I wasn't in good head space," I reluctantly admitted.

Lucky didn't speak for so long, I had to look down at my screen to make sure he hadn't hung up on me.

"You in good head space now?"

"Yeah. Real good."

"You walking?"

"Yeah. I'm in Tennessee. Turns out good old Ronald kidnapped me, or took me away from my mom and twin brother before I was four years old."

"What the fuck?! Are you shitting me?"

"Would I shit my favorite turd?"

Lucky laughed.

"Jesus, Kai, I knew your father was a bastard of epic proportions, but to steal you from your mama and your twin brother, that's just fucking vile."

"Yeah," I agreed.

"What are they like?" he asked.

"My mother died over ten years ago," I whispered. That still hurt to think about. I needed to find out where she was buried. I needed to find out what her favorite flowers were. I needed to...

"Aw, Kai. That bites. What about your brother?"

"He's in the service. He's overseas at the moment. I did a FaceTime talk with him. We're still trying to figure out a way for us to get together."

"Really? Can't he come to where you are? Or, can't you go to where he is?"

"It's a little more complicated than that."

"Well uncomplicate it. He's your family. He's your twin. Figure it out."

I grinned. Damn, I'd missed Lucky.

"I'm calling because I've got another problem."

"Before you get into that, you haven't told me. How are you doing physically?"

"Pretty damn good. I can actually jog, maybe run, but not push it. I can ride a bicycle, no mountain biking. I'm allowed to lift more and more each month."

"Fucking A. That's fucking wonderful!"

"Yeah, the physical therapist I had at Walter Reed was amazing. He was determined to push my ass over the finish line whether I wanted him to or not."

"Now that guy, I'll send him flowers."

I found myself laughing again.

"So what's your other problem?"

"Ronald."

"Don't worry, I'll tell everyone here in Dillingham what happened. If he shows his face anywhere, he'll be in for the beating of his life."

"What do you mean if he shows his face? Aren't you working on his boat?"

"They took it from him. He wasn't making his payments."

"The fishing was that bad?"

"Nah." I could hear the satisfied smile in Lucky's voice. "After your last trip up here, your dad got a lot worse, not even Kenny and Ed could stand him anymore. When he couldn't find a decent crew, he couldn't bring in a decent haul, therefore he couldn't make his payments."

"Shit, Lucky, I would have thought he'd have owned that piece-of-shit boat by now."

"Not the way he drank and whored around. He was constantly taking out mortgages against it. He lost the boat about five months ago. He was lucky they let him take his possessions off her before they padlocked her."

It all came together for me then.

"And that was how he got this bright idea," I muttered.

"What?"

"He's come down here to Jasper Creek and is saying he owns the house that my Mama and brother were making payments on these last twenty years."

"You have got to be kidding me. Wait, never mind. You're not. This is Ronald Davies we're talking about; of course you're not kidding."

"Do you know anybody up there in Dillingham

who might know where he is right now, or how to get in touch with him?"

"Hell, Kai, he's burnt every bridge he ever had. Turns out that woman who home-schooled you was only his second-cousin, not his sister. Those kids of hers hate his ass, so they wouldn't be of any help."

That explained a lot. "I understand."

"I'll check in at the two bars he spent most of his time at. See if anybody there has any ideas."

"I sure would appreciate it."

"Kai, it would be my pleasure. However, if you ever ghost me and the boys like that again, we're going to come find you and kick your ass. We're not going to give a shit if you're disabled or not. Got it?"

I laughed out loud and saw a couple of heads turn my way. "I got it, Lucky."

"Good. I'll call you back."

"Thanks Lucky, I appreciate this."

"You're welcome."

After I hung up with Lucky, I didn't have as much interest in looking up Principal Sykes and Denny Rasmussen. I was too busy thinking about how good I'd had it with the men I had worked with out on the Bering Sea. Ronald might have been a twisted piece of shit, but he'd hired some of the best men in the world.

"Look at you, you're eating that up like a champ."

I stroked Chaos' ears as she licked up the food I'd brought her. She'd been having a nap when I'd first arrived.

"Marlowe, that smells so good that I'd like to eat it," Kizzie said as she bumped her shoulder with mine.

I looked over at the petite veterinarian and smiled. "Don't tell her doctor, but sometimes her mother gives her pumpkin pie which she adores. That's why I found this dog food recipe with pumpkin puree."

"Don't I smell cinnamon?" she asked me.

"Yeah, I put in a little sugar and cinnamon. I figure what the hell, let's make every meal taste like dessert. If I could do that for myself, I sure would."

Kizzie grinned. She reached around me and gently lifted up the bandage on Chaos' side. Chaos whimpered. I started to pet her behind her ear and she settled.

"Her incision is looking good," Kizzie smiled up at me. "She's responding well to her treatment. I think she can go home with you by the end of the week."

"If I have a home," I muttered.

"What?"

"Nothing. Just a little kerfuffle."

"Are you sure?"

"Yeah, Kai's going to get it all straightened out." And wasn't that the weirdest thing in the world? I actually trusted him to do that. I wasn't over here

221

going all control freak, I was actually letting him take care of this thing.

Chaos had stopped eating and her eyes were closing.

"I think lunch time is over with," I said as I eased the bowl away from Chaos' face.

Kizzie nodded. She took the bowl away from me, then handed me a towel to wipe up Chaos' muzzle.

"She's going to be out for a while. All the medication I'm giving her is making her sleepy. That just helps to ensure she doesn't move around all that much and gives her body time to recuperate."

"Makes sense."

"Do you want to come into my office?" Kizzie asked.

I looked down at my watch. I'd been at the animal hospital for three-and-a-half hours. "Let me text Kai and see what's on his schedule."

Kizzie nodded. "I'm going to clean up." She held up the bowl. I nodded. "I'll meet you in reception in a minute or two, and you can let me know your plans."

"Will do," I said.

I was smiling as I walked out to the front of the veterinary clinic. I loved that I was making more and more friends here in Jasper Creek. So far, I hadn't found anyone disagreeable, except maybe that woman with the purple hair who pointed her finger at me. But even she was more funny than annoying.

Leaning against the wall, I looked down at my phone to see if I had missed any texts. I hadn't. I texted Kai and said I was about ready to leave the vet's, but I could also spend more time here if he had something going on. He immediately texted back and said he'd meet me there in a few. I gave him a thumbs up sign, and went to the young man behind the reception desk.

"Can you let me back in so I can talk to Kizzie?"

"Sure."

He hit a buzzer and the door unlocked. I headed back to Kizzie's office.

"No coffee, huh?"

I frowned. "How'd you know?"

"Honey, you have that, 'I'm man crazy' look on your face."

"I do not."

Kizzie laughed. "Okay, you don't."

"Damn. I do, don't I?"

"Yep. So maybe we can meet up for drinks or a meal some other time? I can wrangle in some of the other ladies in town. Do you know Maddie Avery?"

I shook my head.

"She's good people. There's a couple of others in the crew. You'll have fun."

"I'd really like that, Kizzie."

She reached for a card on her desk, then turned it over and wrote something on it and handed it to me. "This is my cell number. I already have yours. Let's try for something next week. Does that work for you?"

"Definitely."

I waved to her and left her office, then left the clinic. Kai's truck wasn't parked in the street, it was tucked near the back of the hardware parking lot. Hell, even here it was nice. They had trees planted, and somebody had planted flowers at the base. Careful not to step on the flowers, I leaned against the tree and looked down at my phone as I soaked in the sun. I needed my vitamin D since I wasn't walking Chaos at least twice a day.

I grinned at the three text messages that had come in from Sue. She said she could only text, because her mouth was killing her. She also explained she was more than capable of listening. I texted back and said that this conversation was a group participation play, so we would have to wait until tomorrow.

I got an immediate reply back. It was the middle finger emoji. Once again I was laughing. Despite the eviction notice, I had to say, it was turning into a pretty good day. Now if I could just jump Kai's bones, it would be a stupendous day.

21

Somebody needs their brakes checked, I thought, as I continued to text with Sue. Damn, she was funny.

Movement caught my eye and I looked up just as someone grabbed my arm holding my phone. He grabbed it *hard.*

"Oww!"

He twisted me around and suddenly my back was pinned against his front. I opened my mouth to yell and he slapped his hand—no not his hand, but something—over my mouth and face.

I couldn't see.

I couldn't breathe.

I kicked backward, trying to hit his shins.

"Shit, bitch, stop it."

His fingers bit tighter into my biceps and this time I yelled in pain. Instead of a scream coming out, a wet cloth and noxious odor was coming into my mouth.

I kicked back again and he lifted me off the ground and spun me around. I tried yelling again, but he shoved the cloth even tighter against my face. I jerked my head back and forth, trying to dislodge it. Doing anything I could to get rid of this...

...smell.

...man.

I needed to...

Kick, Marlowe. Kick.

I tried to kick, but...

I was going to throw-up...

...fight.

...*Kai.*

Hurts. He hurt me...

...*Kai.*

"What in the ever-loving fuck do you think you're doing?" I yelled.

As I came up on the guy who was trying to push Marlowe into the obligatory white panel van I thought my head might explode.

Her ex. Denny. Had to be.

He dropped her and her phone into the van and turned to face me. He reached behind his back, but I didn't have time for this motherfucker to get a gun. He was already dead as far as I was concerned.

I covered the forty feet in less than three seconds and I took him down. I grabbed the gun out of his right hand, then threw it into the flowers. I hit him, and I hit him, and I hit him again.

"Please," the man sputtered, blood spewing. "It's just a job."

I hit him again and again.

"Beau, stop," a man yelled.

"That's Kai," a woman said.

"Whoever he is, he needs to quit—"

"Dave, be quiet and call an ambulance."

Ambulance?

I jumped off the cretin who had been trying to hurt Marlowe and looked around. In the back of the van, I saw Marlowe struggling to get up on her elbows.

"Jesus, Marlowe, are you alright?" I asked as I crawled in beside her.

"I'm."

I carefully embraced her, cradling her head in the crook of my arm.

"You're what, Honey?"

"I think I'm alright." Her words came out slow and slurred.

"How hard did Denny hit you?" I whispered my question.

"That's not Denny."

"It's not?"

"No. I've never seen him before."

Fuck. What in the hell is going on?

I started to press around on the back of her head.

"What are you doing?"

"I'm checking for lumps, to see where he hit you."

"He didn't."

She tried to get away from me, but I wasn't letting her. Fuck, I wasn't going to let her out of my sight again. Next time I was going to be clearer. She was to *stay* in the vet's office, not go wandering around in some parking lot.

"There," she pointed.

I looked to see what she was pointing at. It was a blue rag. When I picked it up I could smell the chloroform. Fuck, he hadn't hit her.

"Where's that ambulance?" I shouted out.

"It's coming." I focused on the woman talking and realized it was Alice Draper, the woman who owned the hardware store with her husband Dave. I took a breath so I wouldn't rip her head off.

"Alice, do you know what the ETA is?"

"It's coming from Sevierville. But I've also called Doc. He should be here in another minute or two."

This time I actually cared, and hoped he was worth a shit. He seemed to be doing okay for Sam, but I hoped he would know how to handle a woman who had just breathed in a bunch of chloroform. Just as I was thinking that, I heard groaning. The scumbag who had hurt Marlowe was coming to.

"Alice, do you think you could keep an eye on Marlowe while I spend a little bit of time with my friend down there?"

"Kai, you don't want to end up in jail," she

cautioned. It was that moment that I realized she was raising teenagers.

"I won't."

Alice clambered into the back of the van and carefully took Marlowe from me, then I jumped out and looked down at the scumsucker. If Nash took him into custody, he'd call for a lawyer, then I wouldn't know who was coming after Marlowe.

I locked eyes with the man who was also standing over the asshole. He held out his hand. "My name is Dave Draper."

I shook it. "Kai. Did you call the sheriff?"

Dave scratched the bottom of his chin. "The way I saw things, that needed to be your call."

I grinned. I was really liking the Drapers.

"So what do you want to do?" he asked.

"I want to take him with me, get some answers out of him, before taking him to Nash."

Dave nodded. "Seems reasonable. No reason to waste the sheriff's time."

I grinned wider.

A burgundy Buick Roadmaster drove right up to us. It had to have been made in the late 1990's. Out came Doc Evans.

"Where's my patient?" He scowled.

"She's in here," Alice called out.

Doc easily climbed into the van. *Man must do some of those PT exercises himself*. I followed him.

"Who the hell's bright idea was it to keep her in

here, and not take her out where there is fresh air?" Doc wanted to know.

Damn, he was right.

Doc picked up the blue rag, took a quick sniff, then threw it out the van door to Dave. "Dispose of this. Preferably where no one else can get to it." He then turned his attention back to me. "Now, let's get her to that bench, out yonder. I don't think she needs oxygen, but I'm going to check her vitals. Somebody call an ambulance?"

I was lifting Marlowe out of the van as Alice was answering the Doc. Dave, however, was not running to dispose of the rag. Instead, his foot was on the neck of Marlowe's assailant. Yep, he was somebody I wanted to go have a beer with. I'd even pay for his.

As soon as I had her on the bench out on the sidewalk, Doc took his stethoscope out along with a blood pressure gauge.

"Honey, your blood pressure is kind of on the low side. What is it normally?"

Marlowe told him.

He gave a satisfied nod.

He then set his stethoscope against her chest. "I want you to breathe normally for me. Can you do that?" Marlowe rolled her eyes. Yep, my girl was feeling better.

"Don't be giving me any of your lip, young lady." He listened to her lungs. "Now I want you to breathe deep for me."

He took the scope away and looked at her. "I take

it he didn't have the rag against you for all that long, did he?"

"No, sir."

"Didn't think so. You're going to end up with quite a headache. You're going to need to go to bed early, and sleep in, but other than that, you should be fit as a fiddle."

"That's it?" I asked.

"That's it." He patted me on the shoulder as he got up off the bench. That's when I noticed we had garnered a little bit of a crowd.

"Nothing here to see, folks. Go about your business."

It was funny to see how everyone obeyed the old doctor. He then turned his attention back to the two of us. "I'm going to tell the ambulance to head back home. There's no need for one. If you find yourself getting dizzy or becoming nauseous, you call me. Alright?"

We both nodded.

"As for the guy on the pavement, am I safe to assume that you're not done with him?" Doc asked me. His whole kindly doctor demeanor had faded away.

"You have assumed correctly."

"Just drop him off with Nash when you're done. He can call in someone from Sevierville to fix him up."

I gave him a chin lift.

Doc got back into his Roadmaster and drove away.

"You good with taking a little bit of a drive?" I asked Marlowe.

"Where are we going?"

"Onyx Security."

She shrugged. "Okay."

When we got back to where her assailant was, things had changed. Instead of the scumsucker being under Dave's boot, he was now on his stomach with his hands and ankles zip-tied.

"Nicely done," I complimented Dave.

"Here." Dave held a gun and a knife. "They're his."

I nodded my appreciation.

"Are you taking him away in his van, or your truck?" Dave asked.

The man was covered in blood, but that wouldn't hurt the bed of my truck. Still, somebody might notice a tied-up man in the back of my truck as I drove to Simon and Roan's office.

"The van," I said.

"Let's get him on up there."

"I can—" I had to stop myself. "Yeah, let's," I ended up saying. It sucked that I needed help. It fucking sucked.

22

I knew Kai was doing something majorly illegal by not getting the sheriff involved with my attacker, but I couldn't really bring myself to care. For that minute that he had me in his grip, I thought I was going to die.

I rolled my head on the passenger seat and looked at Kai's profile. He looked fierce. I could see him on the cover of some Scottish romance novel. He'd be like a warrior with a sword in a kilt, and he'd be faithful only to me.

Want only me.

Forever.

But that was the rub. Where was our relationship going?

It was funny that I thought I needed to talk to Sue. I didn't need to talk to Sue about a damn thing. I knew where my heart was at. It was here. Right here, connected to Kai's. That is, if Kai would have me.

He was nothing like Denny. Kai had only talked me up. He had made me feel like a better version of myself. Plus, he was such. And I mean, *such*. A good guy.

I'd met Sam the one night that I was allowed to bring over dinner. I wasn't sure what to expect. Part of me thought that someone who worked with Pearl for all those years would have had to be a little bit crotchety, but then again, Harvey had hurt his feelings. So I went in with no expectations. What I wasn't expecting was a man with Old World manners and charm. I was stunned he was living alone, but after dinner he took out a photo album and showed me pictures of his wife who had died thirty years ago.

It was after that that he and Kai went into a back bedroom to work on the exercises, and I listened to Kai constantly tell Sam to go easier. Apparently Sam was a lot like Kai—hard on himself, and anxious to get better. No wonder Kai liked him so much.

"Whatcha looking at?" Kai asked softly.

"I'll tell you later." I didn't want to tell him anything gooey when my attacker could overhear.

When we pulled up to the building, Simon Clark and Roan Thatcher came out. I waved to them from the front seat and grinned. Roan came over to the passenger side window and I rolled it down.

"How are you doing, Marlowe?" he asked.

"I'm fine. Doc checked me out. No adverse reactions from the chloroform."

My head whipped around as I heard Simon shout

through the other window. "What the hell Kai, you didn't tell us he hit her with chloroform."

"I was going to. First and foremost, we need some answers," Kai muttered.

Roan opened my door and held out his hand. "Darlin', why don't you go on inside with Betty, and she'll get you set up with whatever you need. If you want snacks, iced tea, soda, beer, whiskey, whatever, she'll set you up."

"She can't have alcohol, are you dumb?" Kai shouted at Roan.

Roan laughed. "She's a big girl, she knows what she can and can't do."

Kai reached across the middle of the van and grabbed my hand. "No alcohol. Not until all of the chloroform is out of your system. Okay?"

I squeezed his hand. "I promise."

"Oh, you've got him wrapped around your little finger, don't you, Darlin'?" Roan chuckled.

I frowned. "I'm the one doing what he says, so I think it's the other way around."

"Didn't you see—" Roan started to say.

"Give it up, Thatcher," Simon broke in. "It'll play out as it's meant to."

They thought they were so smart. I'd met Simon's wife. He was the one who was wrapped around his woman's finger. As for Roan, I hadn't met his woman, but considering the way he was just talking to Marlowe, my guess would be he was just as whipped.

"So what do we have here?" Simon asked as he opened up the side door of the van. I got out so I could stare at Marlowe's would-be kidnapper. Now, besides all the blood dripping on and around his face, there was vomit too. Must not have been a comfortable ride for the bastard.

"This asshole thought it would be nice to kidnap Marlowe outside the hardware store. I thought it was a bad idea, and I made my concerns known."

"Looks like," Roan agreed.

"So you brought him here, why?" Simon asked.

"You seem to have a large building here. I was thinking I could make some use of it and get some of my questions answered before I handed him over to a Nash where he would immediately ask for a lawyer."

"Hey, Simon, he has your number."

Simon glared at Roan.

"Give it up, Boss. Anybody checking out this place is bound to wonder what all this empty space is for and wonder why there isn't a big for rent sign up front."

I glanced over at Simon. "He has you there."

"Is that what made you think I might rent more of this than just our office space?"

"It finally did cross my mind," I admitted.

"Shit," was all Simon had to say about that. "Just

don't mess up the space too badly when you have your talk with your new friend."

"I won't," I promised.

"Why does he get all the fun?" Roan asked. "That doesn't seem fair. The last time I got to ask anybody fun questions was when we were in Baltimore. I'm going to go with Kai."

I looked over my shoulder suspiciously. He didn't look like somebody who was implying I needed help. Which I was going to. I couldn't move this dead weight on my own.

Fuck!

"Have at it. Again, remember to keep it on the linoleum." Simon handed me a set of keys then turned to go back to the office door.

Roan leaned into the van and pulled the unconscious man out, then picked him up and hefted him over one shoulder.

Fuck!

Shut the fuck up, Davies, or Beaumont or whoever the hell you are. You can walk. You can jog. You can run. You can fuck. You have a woman who you love, so just shut the fuck up about those few things you can't do!

"Where do we go?" I asked Simon.

"Around to the back." Roan laughed. "Probably should have had you drive there. Oh well." He hefted the man up a little more.

By the time we got to the back entrance, Roan wasn't even breathing heavy. *Those were the days.*

"My fiancée, Lisa, really likes Marlowe. She's really impressed."

"Were you born and raised here?" I asked.

"Yep. Went to school with Beau. I was a few grades ahead of him. I ran into him a couple of times when we were in the same country, fighting the good fight. Your brother is a good man."

I liked hearing that.

"What brought you back to Jasper Creek?"

"I put my time in and was at that point where I either needed to become a lifer, or go take over the family business, ya know?"

I nodded, like I did know. But I didn't.

"Anyway, I come back here and I find out that my Dad's moved to Florida and my brother might still be in Tennessee, but he doesn't want to have anything to do with our old service shop. The cherry on top is that Dad has put this know-it-all female in charge of the business. He's given her carte-blanche on how to run it."

"Why would he do that if you were going to leave the service and run it?"

"Oh yeah, when I decided to leave the service and come home, I decided to make it a surprise."

"Ah. Fuck."

"It gets worse. Guess who's renting the old family homestead?"

"The know-it-all female?" I ventured.

"You've got it in one."

"What did you do?"

"I ended up proposing." He laughed. "There might have been some other shit that went on between me showing up and me proposing, but the important part is I proposed and she said yes."

I chuckled.

Roan pointed with his head. "There it is. That door."

I moved forward and with the second key I tried, I was able to open the lock. We were in a big storage facility with a cement floor. "Where's the linoleum?"

"We either use the bathroom or the kitchenette. I prefer the kitchenette. More space to move around."

I nodded. Cement was bad because blood had a nasty habit of soaking in, and you weren't able to totally clean it up. Linoleum was easy to clean up.

"Let me down," the guy over Roan's shoulder slurred.

I shut the door and followed Roan to the kitchenette.

"Sure, I'll let you down." Roan dumped him onto the floor. The guy had a hard landing, what with his hands and feet tied up and all.

"Where am I?" He sounded a little less slurred, but he was nasally. I was pretty sure I had broken his nose.

"You're in a place where no one can hear you if you scream. But you won't need to scream as much if you just give us some answers," I told him.

Roan gave me a thumbs up. He was the slightest bit of a goof.

The guy tried to push up into a sitting position, but the way he was tied wouldn't allow it. He dropped back down onto the floor in defeat. "Just ask me what you want to know, and I'll tell you. I don't like this bumfuck town. This was a shit assignment."

"What are you talking about? You're going down for first degree murder," I shouted into his face.

"The fuck I am!" he shouted back, his fear palpable. "I was paid to get answers out of the bitch, not kill her."

"Bullshit. You're the second person who's tried to kill her in the last forty-eight hours," I yelled back. If I didn't need him to answer questions, I would put my boot through his skull.

"No, man. No. I can prove it. The old man told me himself. I was to get her phone, and I was to find out where she has her shit backed up. I was to find the video. If I had to hurt her to get the information, that was okay. But I needed to make sure all of the copies were gone, and bring him her phone."

"What in the fuck are you talking about?" Roan interrupted.

"Check the van if you don't believe me. Her phone was still rolling around in the back when you took me."

I nodded my head at Roan and he left to go check things out.

"Now what fucking video are you talking about? And who is your client?"

"The senator. He called me in late last night. He

said some other guy screwed the pooch and almost killed the teacher, which is not what the senator needed to have happen. Then the senator lays it all out to me. The teacher has a video on her phone that he needs."

"What kind of video is it?" I was confused.

"I don't fucking know. It was some asshole kids. Girls. Bullying some other asshole kids. Girls. Anyway, all those snowflakes got their dicks in a ringer, and somebody taped it or something and the senator wants to make sure he has every copy."

"So he sent *you*?"

"I used to work at Blockbuster back in the day. I told him, I was an expert at getting things erased."

"So you were going to get her to delete her entire back-up account? How were you going to make sure it wasn't archived somewhere else?"

He gave me a dumbfounded look.

"Fine, tell me who this senator is."

"Teddy Thompson, District Eighteen in West Virginia."

"And how are you supposed to get in touch with Teddy when you accomplish your mission?"

"I'll call him, and then we'll set up a time where we can meet up and I can give him the phone."

"Have you met each other before?"

He shook his head.

"Well okay then."

23

"Let's go."

Kai was holding out both of his hands. One had my phone in it, the other was clearly for me to take. I took it.

"Good-bye, Betty. I would definitely love to meet up with your reading group sometime."

I could barely get those words out of my mouth before Kai was dragging me out of the Onyx offices. When we got outside, I winced. I desperately needed my sunglasses; the bright sun was already giving me a headache.

"Are you alright?" Kai stopped marching forward and placed his palm against my cheek.

"I'm fine. What's the rush?"

"Never mind the rush. Are you okay?"

"The sun's hurting my head," I muttered.

His thumb brushed back and forth along my jaw.

"Fuck, I should have thought of that. Your purse is in my truck."

"No, it's not. It's in the hardware store parking lot," I protested.

"Sweetheart, my truck is right over there," he pointed.

I squinted and saw that Dave Draper was standing beside his truck, and Alice was standing next to a Prius. "Dave and Alice helped us out and brought my truck over here, so I could drive you to the hospital, or home, or wherever."

"Home?"

Oh no. I hadn't even thought about home. Kai must have seen the pain on my face. He pulled me gently into his arms. "Marlowe, it's all going to be alright."

"But I like my home." My words were so soft I knew he couldn't hear.

"I like your home too. And you will not have to leave it," he whispered back to me. "That whole eviction thing is bull-doo-doo."

I choked out a laugh. "Don't make me laugh. It hurts."

"Let's get your sunglasses out of your purse and get you into my truck with the AC blowing. How does that sound?"

"Can we get dessert someplace? I deserve a treat."

"Marlowe, you can get whatever your heart desires."

This time, I kept my laughter inside. What would he say if I told him he was what my heart desired?

"Thanks, Dave," Kai said as he held open the passenger seat door. Kai bent inside, grabbed my purse, and handed it to me. I fumbled with the clasp. The headache that Doc had warned me about was coming on strong and my fingers were all thumbs.

I shoved my purse at Kai. "Here, you find my glasses."

He just held my purse and stood there like an ice sculpture. "Open it," I prodded.

"Your purse?" he asked.

Dave grabbed it out of his hands, opened my purse, and plucked out my glasses, then handed them to me. "Don't mind him. Bachelors are scared shitless of a woman's purse. It took Alice five years to get me over my fear."

Kai took my purse from Dave, who was laughing, and then Kai helped me up into the passenger seat and put my purse onto my lap. I slipped my phone into my purse and he shut the door. I saw Kai saying something to Dave, but I couldn't hear it. Then Kai jogged around to the driver's seat and came in.

"How bad is your headache?" he asked after he got the truck out onto Hwy 321.

"I need some ibuprofen and sugar pretty darn fast. I should have asked Betty if she had any. It was my bad."

"Marlowe, no beating up on my girlfriend, okay?"

I turned my head to look at him, but he was

staring out the windshield. Then his hand reached over and grabbed mine, and he tangled our fingers together. I felt myself melt, despite the blasting air conditioning.

"Girlfriend?" I finally asked.

"I've got to say, I'd prefer calling you my woman, but I wasn't sure how that would fly."

My fingers squeezed his tighter. "If it's just you and me, I like that just fine. Because I sure as hell would like to be able to call you my man."

I watched as a smile spread across his face. Ooh, this was a better look than the brooding Scottish warrior romance cover. Hmm, maybe he could be a hot next-door-neighbor-type that goes from friends to lovers. Yeah, that would work.

"So have you decided?"

"Huh?" What was he talking about? He didn't know about my romance cover fetish, did he?

"Is it sugar, or ibuprofen?"

Oh. That. "Ibuprofen," I answered.

I watched as he hit a button on his steering wheel, and the name Pearl's popped up on his dashboard display.

After two rings somebody picked up and said, "Pearl's."

"This you, Pearl?" Kai asked.

"Yeah, who's asking?" She did not sound all that pleasant.

"It's Kai Davies."

"Well, hey, Kai. Why didn't you say so from the

start?" Now she sounded almost motherly. "Are you stopping by for dinner tonight? It's on the house, you know."

"I need to know if you have ibuprofen there."

"Of course we do. It's in the first aid kit. You have a headache?"

"Marlowe does. Somebody tried to kidnap her and used chloroform on her. Doc said she'd probably have a headache. But Marlowe also wants something sweet."

"Kidnap her?" Pearl screeched. "You hustle your buns over here. I'll take care of poor Marlowe."

The line went dead.

"We're going to eat at Pearl's tonight," Kai said.

"Works for me."

Hell, everything worked for me. I was Kai Davies' woman!

"What do you mean, you were evicted? That can't be right. Beau wouldn't evict you, would he?"

I think someone was talking to me, but Marlowe was using her straw to scoop up the whipped cream off her milkshake and daintily lick the cream off the tip. I was breaking out in a cold sweat as I watched her.

She's hurt. No sex.

She's been injured. No sex.

She's been scared. No sex.

"Kai, are you listening to me?"

I looked away from Marlowe to see Pearl glaring at me. "Tell me your brother would not evict our sweet Marlowe. Tell me."

"It wasn't Beau. It was our father."

"Arthur?" Pearl screeched again.

Out of the corner of my eye, I saw Marlowe wince. She was seated right next to Pearl, the same woman who had taken our orders, delivered our food, then promptly sat down at our booth and demanded to know everything that had happened.

"Pearl, you've gotta keep it down. Marlowe has a headache, remember?"

"Oh yeah, the chloroform." She nodded. She turned to look at Marlowe who plunked her straw back into her milkshake. "Are you okay, baby?"

"I could probably go for a piece of pie," Marlowe said. "To go."

"Sure. What kind?"

"Surprise me," Marlowe said. She winked at me as Pearl hurried away to get Marlowe her pie.

"So, where are we staying tonight, my man?" Marlowe asked. Her voice was a low purr. "Are we staying in Randy's room? Your suite, or my rented house that could have all of my possessions thrown out on the front lawn."

"First off, I've called Nash. The person in charge of throwing your possessions out on the front lawn would be the sheriff. Guess who doesn't intend to do that?"

"The sheriff?" Marlowe guessed.

"My woman gets a gold star." I saw her wiggle in her seat as I used the phrase, 'my woman.' It seemed she got off on it. Good to know.

"In that case, I would really like to introduce you to my sheets," Marlowe whispered.

"I would love that introduction."

Kai was being amazingly difficult to seduce. It was past the point of irritation and was now beginning to piss me off. When we'd first arrived at Onyx, I'd gone into the bathroom and cleaned up as best I could. Then when I got home, I'd brushed my teeth, brushed my hair, washed my face, and brushed on some mascara and lip gloss, so I knew I didn't look like a swamp creature. But still, no go. And that was after I had played with him at Pearl's with the whole milkshake, whipped cream, straw thing.

What the hell?

We were on the couch; I was snuggled up to the corner, with one leg tucked up beneath my fanny, and the other hanging off the edge. Kai was in the middle, looking at me. He was telling me some hilarious stories about the guys he had served with. I was with him. I really, really hoped that Clay would find himself a girlfriend. But more than that, I wanted to get Kai into my bedroom.

I had been touching his leg. Touching his shoulder. Touching his arm. Making sure that my t-shirt collar hung down as far as it would go so that he could see ta-ta. Sue always said that showing ta-ta would get me somewhere, but apparently not tonight.

"Honey, sex is not on the table tonight."

What?

What-what?

"What did you just say?"

"Marlowe, I need you to know that making love to you has been the highlight of my life."

"Why do I hear a but coming on? Are you dumping me?"

Kai reached over and grabbed me. In a flash I was on his lap. "You're kidding, right?"

"Uhm. I don't know," I said quietly. "That kind of sounded like the start of a break-up speech. Everything has gone so fast for us in the last twenty-four hours, so I thought maybe..."

"You're thinking wrong. Marlowe, we've been seeing each other for five weeks. Yeah, the last twenty-four hours has been intense, but why would I want to break up with you?"

I shook my head. I didn't want to answer that question. How did you say, *I'm kind of fucked up in the head?*

"Let's go back to where you were saying that sex with me was the highlight of your life." I put a wide smile on my face.

"Marlowe, you weren't listening. I didn't say sex, I

said making love. I said what I meant. Seeing that man with his hands on you? Seeing you passed out in that van? That has a tendency to make a blind man see."

Insecurity mixed in with this headache meant that I was not the brightest tool in the shed. Or maybe Kai just wasn't saying things straight. Either way, I was frustrated as fuck!

"Just say what you mean."

Great, I sound like an angry fishwife.

Kai laughed. "I'm not saying this right. Marlowe, you mean the world to me."

"But…"

"Stop it, woman! What I'm trying to say is that today scared the shit out of me, and it smacked me in the face that I was head-over-heels in love with you. My life wouldn't be worth living if I didn't have you in it."

In love with you.

He kept talking, but all that kept rattling around in my head was that he was *in love with me*. This guy. This *real* guy. This wonderful man. He was in love with me. And he was *real*.

Aw shit, I could feel the first tear trailing down my cheek. What the hell? I didn't cry! What was going on?

"Sweetheart, say something."

I struggled out of his arms to go get a tissue.

"Marlowe, where are you going?"

"Tissues," I mumbled.

"I'll get them. You stay right here."

He came back in just a moment with the box. How had he known where the tissues were?

Focus!

I took four out of the box and pressed them up to my face, trying to stop the fountain of tears, but it felt like a big plug had been pulled out, and my crying was never going to stop.

I found myself back in the crook of Kai's arm. As if he were cradling me. He was stroking the hair away from my face and kissing my forehead, the curve of my jaw, and whispering silly things in my ear.

Silly, silly, things.

"I love you, Marlowe."

"You're precious to me."

"I love your dog."

"I want to build a life with you, Sweetheart."

Silly, silly, things.

24

I woke up alone in my bed. It was my bed, I recognized my yellow sheets. I didn't want to get up. I was scared to. I needed to think. Had yesterday really happened? I rolled over and saw a note on the pillow where I was pretty sure Kai had slept. The note was written on a paper towel. I grinned.

Marlowe –
Gone back to the hotel. I'm checking out, just like you suggested. I'll be back with my gear after I stop off at Onyx and the Sheriff's office.
I love you,
Kai

I vaguely remembered telling him to get his shit and move in already. Thank God I did; saved me from having to work up the courage to tell him to do it today.

I rolled over to my side to get out of bed and found that Kai had even put my phone in my charger.

Now I *had* to keep him.

I looked at my phone and saw that Sue had already texted me twice this morning. Time to put my best friend out of her misery.

I pushed in her number.

"It's about damned time you answered your phone! I was about to get on a plane."

"As if, Little Pixie, like your husband would allow you to come out for a visit without him."

"You're right, he wouldn't. Therefore, I would have back-up when I held you down on the floor and beat the information from you."

I shuddered. Not the best image at the moment.

"How about we stop with that line of teasing for the moment, until we're caught up?"

"Marlowe?" Sue's voice was quiet. "Has something happened since yesterday morning's text?"

God, she knew me well. She could pick up on just my tone that fast that something wasn't right. I loved this woman.

"A ton of good stuff. Some scary stuff. But mostly good," I rushed to assure her.

"Okay." She drew the word out so it was five syllables. "Tell me the 'not good' and scary stuff first."

253

"What makes you think there is 'not good' stuff, too?"

"Not good goes hand-in-hand with scary, so fess up."

"We made love!"

"You and Kai, not me and you, right? Just for clarification. I teach English, so it's important that we get this conversation started off correctly."

I laughed. "Yes, me and Kai. Or is it Kai and I? Whatever, we made love. I said we had sex, but he said we made love!"

I heard her gasp.

"He said that? The muscularly, soldierly, kind of grim guy?"

"The grim part was early on. I've seen him grin and smile and even chuckle now. And Sue, you should hear him laugh. He has the best laugh."

"Did he laugh when you made love?"

I paused.

"He did." I thought some more. "Was that bad? I didn't think it was bad at the time. We were both laughing. So I thought—"

"Stop already, I was teasing. Yes, laughter is good, and I'm going to hunt down Denny Rasmussen and kick his ass...again."

That made me laugh, too. "Okay, let me tell you more. The scary stuff is I was almost kidnapped, but that wasn't as scary as almost being driven off the road over a cliff. That had been much scarier, but apparently chloroform is really bad for you. I'm still preferring the botched kidnapping, plus that way Chaos didn't get hurt and—"

"STOP!"

"What?"

"STOP ALREADY!"

I thought over what I had just said. "I hadn't told you about being almost run off the road, had I?" My tone was meek.

"No. No, you haven't. You think you might want to back up just a minute and start over?"

I heard muttering in the background.

"You made me wake up Angie with my yelling. Steve is going to expect free babysitting from you in the future."

"Okay. Done deal."

"Okay, you're driving along with Chaos as your co-pilot, and then what?" Sue asked.

"A truck rear ends me. You would have thought that would have been the end of it, but we were on this big downhill road with a cliff on one side and a rock wall on the other. The truck keeps trying to push me off over the cliff. Luckily, I got away, but Chaos is hurt."

I cross my fingers that I've said enough to satisfy her. Kai didn't let me get away with that tiny amount of detail. Oh no, he insisted on a blow by excruciating blow of what had happened. He got grumpier by the second. Come to think of it, he was probably over at the sheriff's office wanting to know where that truck and driver were at this very minute.

"How bad was Chaos hurt?" Sue asked.

"Really bad. She needed surgery. She has to stay at the vet for another four or five days. I'm cooking her food and bringing it over. While my 4Runner is impounded, Kai is chauffeuring me around and taking me over to the vet's so I can love on Chaos."

"Ohhh."

Yeah, that scored Kai some points.

"Now tell me about the chloroform," Sue demanded.

"Don't you want to know about Greek God sex? Actually, he's more Highland Warrior sex."

"Woman, I have my own Highland Warrior…who happens to be within earshot, so we can dispense with that part of today's story time. Instead, get on with the kidnapping."

"What kidnapping?" Steve rumbled in the background.

"Somebody tried to kidnap Marlowe," Sue said.

"Put the phone on speaker," Steve demanded.

"Hey, Marlowe," Steve greeted me.

"Hey, Steve."

"Now talk." That was Sue.

"The kidnapping was a big bust. I was waiting by Kai's truck for him to come and meet me. It was a guy in a white panel van. No kidding, it was a for-real white panel van. Anyway, he pulls up, opens the door, and tries to pull me in."

"And what, you're just standing there, waiting like

the Christmas goose or something?" Sue wanted to know.

"Actually, I was texting you."

"Figures," Steve mumbled.

"He puts a rag with chloroform over my mouth, and I start to pass out. The next thing I remember is seeing this guy on the pavement with Kai straddling him and beating the bejesus out of him."

"Good man," Steve muttered. "I like him already."

"So, this happened to you within two days?" Sue asked for clarification. "Do you know why?"

"Yeah. It turns out Cindy Thompson's dad, the state senator, wanted all copies of the video that she made. She must have told her dad that I sent one to my phone."

"How'd you find that out?"

"Before turning the kidnapper over to the sheriff, Kai decided to have a little chat with him and get some answers."

"I'm really, *really* liking this guy," Steve reiterated. "So, what does he do for a living?"

"He's retired military."

"Why'd he retire in Jasper Creek?"

"That's the problem. I'm not sure that he has."

"What do you mean, you're not sure? Where does he live?" Steve continued with his questioning. Apparently, Sue hadn't been keeping him up to date.

"Kai was only here to look up his long-lost brother. They only made contact a little bit ago."

"But he's been there long enough for you to fall in

love with him?" Steve asked. He was starting to sound grumpy.

"Yeah, he's been here for five weeks."

"I'm not catching on here, Marlowe. If he's been there for five weeks, where's he been living?"

"In a hotel, but I told him last night to come live here with me. But I don't know if that'll work, because his dad just sent a server to evict me."

"What!" Sue shouted.

I heard Angie whimper.

"I'm tapping out," Steve said. "But Sue, you better have answers to make sense of all of this after I get Baby Girl her breakfast."

"I will," Sue promised her husband.

"I'll make this quick," I promised Sue. "I got an eviction notice from Arthur Beaumont. That is Beau Beaumont's dad who has been gone from Jasper Creek for twenty years. According to what the sheriff found out, he must have the deed to the house, but that can't be right, since Mrs. Beaumont, his wife, and Beau Beaumont, her son, had to have been making all the mortgage payments, so it belonged to them."

"So is Arthur Beaumont also Kai's dad?"

"Yes. Kai has been asking his friends up in Alaska about where he might be. So far nobody knows anything."

"Do you have to leave your house?"

"Not according to Kai or the sheriff, so I'm staying put."

There was a long pause.

"Marlowe, I've known you for ten years now. Back to our university days."

I braced. "I know."

"I've known you through the Denny years."

"I know."

"This has got to be the scariest, craziest most, screwed-up shit I've ever heard."

"I know."

"But you know something?" Sue asked.

"What?"

"I've never heard you sound happier."

25

"It's about damn time you called me back, old man," I growled into the phone.

"For someone who leaves a message saying they need help, that's a piss-poor way to start a conversation," Bernie responded. The asshole didn't even sound perturbed.

"Yeah, well, I just got a blast from the past, and the only time I would have liked to have heard about or seen this guy again was if I had an opportunity to spit on his grave."

"Arthur," Bernie said with disgust.

"Yep. And he's causing trouble."

"That's one of his specialties. Another couple of them are greed and cruelty."

"Those fit. He's filed an Unconditional Quit Notice on Beau's house. It states that Marlowe is living in the house unlawfully because he's the owner."

"Are you fucking kidding me?" Bernie demanded.

"Nope. You need to get Beau on the line and tell him what's happening."

"Wait a minute. Wait one goddamned minute. What right does Arthur say he has to declare hisself the owner?"

"Simon Clark says he'll have the court documents today. Not through normal channels. But he'll have them. Anyway, what the county clerk said is that he has the deed to the property."

"Something he had made up at some one-hour-copy-shop, knowing that old bastard," Bernie grumbled.

"Did you know my dad?" I asked. I'd never thought to ask Bernie that before.

"Sorry, kid, talking out of turn. When I said knowing that old bastard, I was just basing it on what others had said about him. I got here when Beau was about fourteen years old. Went fishing with him more than a few times. Quiet kid. I liked him."

"How'd you end up acting as his rental agent?"

"It was about the time I was renting out my old cabin that Beau's Mama— Sorry, I mean your Mama —passed. He was getting ready to go into the service. We were out fishing and he was talking about selling the house, and I didn't want to see him cut all ties with Jasper Creek. I felt like he'd regret it in the end. Especially with Maddie and all."

"Maddie?"

"That's a long story. Anyway, I talked him into

keeping the house and I promised he'd make money on it every year. Hell, I even made sure he re-financed it when he could, so he'd get better loan rates. So, the idea that Arthur owns the house is utter bullshit."

"Do you have that paperwork?" I asked.

"Fuck no. That wasn't for me to keep. That was Beau's paperwork. I would send that mail to him at Pendleton, out in California. That's where he's based. Not that it does him any good. Swear to God, he's hardly ever there."

God, do I understand that.

I wonder if he ever tires of the life?

"Okay, well, you explained it all," I agreed. "But without the paperwork and without Beau, it looks like Arthur is holding the winning hand."

"Not on my watch," Bernie declared. "And it sure as shit shouldn't be on your watch."

I smothered a grin. I was seriously, seriously, seriously liking the people in this town, more and more.

"I'm not giving up the ship. Marlowe and I aren't moving out."

"Oh, so you're shacked up now, are you?"

"We don't have time to gossip. I need you to have Beau FaceTime me. Tell me his number, so I can put it in my phone."

"Hey, that's not our standard operating—"

"I'm his twin, for fuck's sake. Tell me his number."

Bernie gave me Beau's number.

"Now tell me about Maddie."

Bernie chuckled. "We don't have time to gossip," he repeated my words back to me.

I laughed. "It was worth a try."

I met Simon at the sheriff's office. The officer at the front desk led us back to Nash's office. He stood up behind his desk and gave us both a chin lift.

"Harry, close the door behind them, okay?"

"Yes, sir."

The three of us waited for the door to close before we sat down.

"So, what have you found out from the kidnapper?" Simon asked.

"Funny, that was going to be my question for the two of you." Nash squinted at Simon. It was as if the two of them had locked horns in the past.

"It's not me you should look at. I didn't touch him. You need to talk to the town's lost son. What do you say, Kai? Feel like sharing with the long arm of the law?" Simon smirked my way.

I shrugged. "He admitted his assignment wasn't to kill her, he was just supposed to get her phone from her and erase all recordings and back-ups of a video she had on her phone."

"What the hell? This doesn't make any sense," Nash bit out.

"He said that the person who had hired him was a

state senator from West Virginia. Teddy Thompson, Eighteenth District."

"Well, that's just great," Nash said sarcastically. "Because I'm getting absolutely nothing. I have someone with a rap sheet as long as my arm, with an attorney whose hourly rate is more than his monthly rent. I think it's safe to say that our friend Teddy is paying for his defense, wouldn't you say?"

Simon and I both nodded.

"We're not going to get the senator on jack-shit." Nash sounded utterly disgusted.

"The only other way this was going to play out, Rivers, was that you were going to take him into custody, he would have demanded a lawyer, same suit would have come in, and you wouldn't have known about Teddy Thompson. Don't sit there all sanctimonious like this is an us problem," Simon drawled. "We actually did you a favor."

"Oh yeah, this is a big-time favor. I have some asshole in my jail, that is going to be let out on bail on Monday, and I can't do jack about it. Meanwhile, the guy behind it all goes scot free."

I figured it was my turn to speak up.

"I talked to Marlowe last night. She was still out of it because of the chloroform, but she explained to me why Teddy wants her phone. The long and short of it is, Teddy's daughter could be brought up on assault charges for what she did to a student that she was bullying. According to Marlowe, the bigger problem for the senator would be for his daughter to be branded a bully. Bad for his reputation."

"That's not true. Tell me that's not true. You're saying Marlowe almost gets killed on Amber Road, then someone tries to kidnap her, and it's all so some fucking state senator's daughter won't be outed as a bully?" Nash looked outraged.

"I'm just as baffled as you are," I told Nash.

Simon sat up straight in his chair and crossed his arms. "I choose to believe that the fact that all three of us are confused makes us better people. And that's how I'm going to raise all my kids."

"All your kids? Not just Bella?" Nash asked. "You got something to tell us?"

Simon fidgeted for just a moment. "Apparently, I'm not supposed to tell people before the first trimester. That's next week. But it's been killing me. So yeah. Trenda and I are expecting."

Nash stood up and came around his desk to pound Simon on his shoulder. "That is great news, Simon. Fantastic news. Trenda must be thrilled to death, and Bella must be over the moon."

"We haven't told Bella yet. When we do, it'll be all over town in a day."

"You got that right." Nash chuckled. Then he looked over at me. "So, what are we going to do about the lawyered-up asshole in my jail?"

"I don't see any way of turning him against the senator, just process him through," I answered.

"Agreed." Nash grimaced. "In the meantime, we're

still on the lookout for the asshole who tried to run Marlowe off the road."

"I doubt you'll find him. Besides running away from you, he's also running away from the senator. He had the same job as the guy in your lock-up. Grab the phone, get rid of the copies. But instead, he tries to kill her. Not too bright," I said. "I'm still worried about the senator. He hasn't accomplished what he's wanted. That means Marlowe is still in danger."

Simon and Nash both nodded.

"Where is she now?" Nash asked.

"In the safest place I could think of leaving her."

"Little Grandma, that didn't really happen, did it?" I asked. Not for the first time, either. This woman was telling me things that were blowing my mind.

"Just because I'm up there in age, doesn't mean that I didn't live a well-lived life. And that includes a little bit of titillation."

She looked like a sweetie pie sitting there on the other side of the table, sipping her warm mug of tea and nibbling on her biscuit. Finding out that she got a job as a tourist guide at the Great Smoky Mountains National Park in 1942 was fascinating. Even more interesting was finding out about all of the people she got to meet. Most of the eligible bachelors in Jasper Creek and all the surrounding areas were trying to help keep their family farms afloat or they had joined or had been drafted into military service.

"It was slim pickings back in the day, let me tell you. I was the oldest, at twenty-two, and let me tell you, Gladiola, Ronnie, and Winnie wouldn't let me forget it. I was definitely an old-maid. They picked on me relentlessly."

"What is your name?" it finally occurred to me to ask.

"Esperance. Our family was French. Our last name was Dubois."

"Esperance is a lovely name." It really was. "Does it mean something?"

"It means hope. I guess they were hopeful when they had me. My parents didn't know they were going to end up with seven daughters. But Ma and Pa took it in stride. Even though we couldn't work the land, they always had hope and faith that things would work out."

"Seven daughters? Why are you only mentioning three other sisters?"

"We were the oldest. The others were still at home. We were the ones who were out in the big wide world trying to bring home money to support the family. We all made money at the Park. I was a guide. Ronnie did clerical work at the Parks Management office then Gladiola and Winnie worked at the concession stands."

"I can't imagine there being many tourists during the war," I said.

"You'd be surprised. I think it was because of the war that more people wanted to go out and visit places. Take a few days and see nature. Commune with God." Little Grandma took another sip of her tea.

"Do you mind if I steal my woman from you?"

We both looked up to see Kai standing over our table. How had I missed him?

"Absolutely. I was wondering why you would be leaving such a beautiful woman alone on such a sunny day," Little Grandma grinned up at Kai.

"You'd best be taking Esperance out for a drive," I said to Kai. He frowned for less than a second, then held his hand out to Little Grandma.

"My chariot awaits, milady. Have you been to Java Jolt? They have some exceptional flavors of coffee."

Little Grandma gave him a broad smile. "I like you, Kai Davies. You'll do. You'll do just fine." She turned to me. "Now go on with yourself. You and your young man have a good time."

"I expect to hear more about your adventures at the Great Park," I told her as I slipped out of my seat.

"You will, my dear."

26

My hands were practically shaking as I opened the door to Marlowe's house.

"Are you okay?" she asked.

"No. Not really. How's your head?"

"My head's fine." She walked over to where my backpack was lying on her dining room table, then looked over her shoulder at me. "So, you're moved in?"

"My duffel is in your bedroom, so yeah. I'm moved in."

She slowly grinned. "Does this mean we're officially shacked up?"

I winced. "I'm not sure I like that term. It's what Bernie said, too."

Marlowe smiled wider. "It's true."

"Let's get something straight. I'm taking over the rent."

She laughed out loud. "Do you have a job?"

"Not at the moment. But I have my pension and a nest egg."

"Why don't you let me continue to pay for things as is, until you get a job?"

"Uh-uh. Not going to happen, otherwise my shit's going back to the Pines."

"Fine," she huffed. "It's fifty-fifty, straight down the line. Except when you ask to take me out someplace, then you can pay."

"Deal. For the moment. We can renegotiate after I get a job."

"Little Grandma said they were hiring."

I sauntered over to my woman and grabbed her around the waist. "Thanks for always thinking about me," I whispered in her ear.

"That's how the game is played. I worry about you, you worry about me. We're a team." She looked up into my eyes, questioning. "Right?"

"That's absolutely right. We're a team. I told you last night where I stand. What about you? Are you all in?"

She wrapped her arms around my waist. "Damn right I am. I love you."

I let out a deep breath.

"What? You knew that already, didn't you?"

"You hadn't said the words," I whispered.

She pulled back so she had a better look at me. "Sure, I did, last night, when we were on the couch. I told you how I felt."

I chuckled. "Honey, you were out of your head

with a headache and the after effects of chloroform. Trust me, I would have remembered if you'd said you'd loved me."

She pulled me in tighter. Chest to breast, then leaned up on her tiptoes and kissed the underside of my chin. "I love you so much, Kai. I don't know how I existed in this world without you. You make the sun shine brighter. I feel safe with you."

I snorted. "Yeah sure. You almost die on Amber Road, then you're almost kidnapped."

She put her fingers to my lips. "Do you know what I was thinking when that scum had me in his van?

I shook my head.

"I didn't think it. I knew it. Deep down, I knew that you were going to save me. I knew it to my bones. You're my hero."

Something clicked in me. It was like all the broken parts of me somehow pieced themselves back together with a resounding snap. She'd put me back together with her words. I felt like me again. A whole man.

I bent down and brushed my lips against hers. I needed to kiss this woman who had come to mean the world to me. This woman who could weave magic with her words.

Marlowe didn't hesitate. She moved, and her hands were caressing my cheeks as she opened her mouth to invite me in. Soon I was tasting the flavor of Marlowe, the heady essence that could send me to the moon and back. This time when I couldn't carry her to the bedroom, I didn't even flinch. It didn't bother me in the slightest. This was my new normal, and it didn't make me less than.

I put my arm around her shoulders, and she put her arm around my waist.

"You don't make your bed," I teased.

"Why would I do that? I'm just going to get back into it later that night. Seems like a waste of effort to me. Do you make your bed?"

"Every morning."

"Freak." She giggled.

I pushed her down onto the unmade bed and she continued to giggle. I started taking off my clothes and she knelt up on the bed, taking off her clothes too. Apparently, it became a race. I hoped she'd win. That would mean I had the most Marlowe naked time.

"You're sure the headache is gone?" I asked as I went to my duffel to grab condoms.

"If I still had it, this would be the perfect remedy."

I turned and squinted at her.

"Stop it. The headache is gone. I promise you. Want sex. Now. Remember?"

I hesitated.

"Look, ta-tas." She lifted up her full, firm breasts.

"I'm looking." I dumped the strip of condoms on her nightstand and tugged her down so that we were both lying next to one another. Her beautiful brown eyes were dancing with mirth.

"What are you looking at?"

"You. Just you." I went in for another kiss. Soon I was lost. Just being connected to her in a kiss had me forgetting that we were naked in a bed. But when Marlowe grabbed my ass, I remembered the plot. I broke away from her mouth and started to string biting kisses downward.

"Oh goodness. You're good at this."

"No, Sweetheart. We're good at this. Trust me, this is a we thing." Her eyes fluttered shut as I licked at the pulse point on her neck. Her heart was beating a mile a minute. Soon I was confronted with her beautiful breasts. Ta-tas. What a silly word for something so miraculous. As I licked all around the tip of her nipple, I reveled in her whimpers of pleasure. Then I took her pointed nub into my mouth and she let out a loud sigh.

"Yes. Just like that."

I continued my ministrations. I used my right hand to tease her other breast.

"Yes. So perfect."

That was my line. She was so perfect.

I trailed my left hand down. Past her bellybutton, until I got to the good stuff. I found her soaked.

Marlowe spread her legs, eager for my touch. Yet another thing that made me feel ten-feet-tall. I speared two fingers into her hot, tight channel and she bucked upwards, her soft body hitting my hard, aching cock. *Game over.*

I removed my fingers and licked them. She was

watching every move I made, and me licking her essence off my fingers turned her on. I grabbed for a condom off the nightstand, tore it open and rolled it on as fast as I could.

"I wanted to do that," she pouted.

"Maybe next year, when I have more control around your naked body," I promised.

Her sultry grin did nothing to help my self-control.

"Are you ready?" I asked.

"I don't know. Weren't you the one testing the waters?"

I barked out a laugh. "I guess I was. Yep, you're ready."

Marlowe's bruises were now green and yellow, so I rested most of my body weight onto my one fore-arm, as I guided my penis to her delicate entrance. Just like the times before, she reared upwards, taking more of me than I was ready to give.

My woman was greedy.

My woman was perfect.

I thrust the rest of the way inside of her body, and my groan of pleasure mirrored her moan. I stayed there. Not moving. Basking in the way we fit together. Marlowe opened her eyes and looked at me from beneath her lashes. Then the minx squeezed me. I groaned again.

"You're not going to go easy on me, are you?"

"What's the fun in that?" she purred.

She had a point.

I pulled out the tiniest bit and thrust back in. I did it two more times in quick succession.

"Now who's not going easy?" She gasped.

"All's fair."

She clamped down on me again, and my grin matched hers. Just like that, I was riding the best ride in the amusement park.

Our bodies were soon slick with desire as we fought to bring each other to the brink. Back and forth we played with one another. She tried to push me over onto my back. I made her work for it before I acquiesced. Her smile of triumph was a thing of beauty.

"I've gotcha now," she crowed.

"Yeah, but what are you going to do with me?" I smirked.

"This." She rose up, then slammed down on my cock, then she bit my chest.

God, this woman was made for me.

I rolled her back over and nuzzled her neck as I thrust in and out, I could tell I was hitting that magical spot inside of her, because her moans were getting serious.

"Kai. Do something," she begged.

"I thought I was," I teased.

"More. Make it more. Kai. Do more."

I loved the way she wasn't making sense. Hell, I was about close to gibberish, that's the reason I wasn't talking. I pressed in deeper, making sure to twist my hips. Each time I did, Marlowe would gasp, or moan, or cry out. Each sound she made would push me closer to the edge.

"I'm close. So close," she whispered.

Thank God.

I thrust deep.

"Yes! God yes."

Her channel gripped me like a vice, and I went over the same hill of the rollercoaster.

"Fuck, yeah."

We were both reading on the sofa when my phone played Lynard Skynyrd's "Free Bird." Marlowe looked up at me, a question in her gaze.

"That's Beau," I answered her unasked question.

"Say hi for me."

I nodded. Then went to the dining room table and picked up my phone. It was still a shock to see a variation of my face staring back at me.

"Bernie said there's a problem. What is it?"

"I'm good, brother, thanks for asking. How are you?"

"Fuck that, Brady. Tell me what's going on."

"The name is Kai."

Beau sighed. I watched as he squeezed the bridge of his nose. Weird. Apparently some things were just genetics.

"Okay, Kai. How are you? What's the weather like?" Beau paused. "Do you feel all warm and snuggly now? Can you tell me what the fuck is going on?"

"Marlowe was served papers. It was an Unconditional Quit Notice. Basically it means—"

"I know what it means. It's bullshit. I didn't file it, and I'm the owner. Ignore it."

"Not quite that easy. The person who filed it, did it with the county clerk's office. They must have shown up with the deed to the house."

"That's impossible."

I could see Beau getting red in the face. Time to cut to the chase.

"It was filed on behalf of Arthur Beaumont," I told him.

Beau stared at me for almost thirty seconds. "You're not kidding me, are you?" he whispered.

"No. I'm not."

"Your father—"

"Our father," I interrupted him.

"Okay, our father. That fucking bastard has the nerve to come to Tennessee after twenty years with some bogus piece of paper and pretend like he owns a house that my mom—"

"Our mom," I interrupted again.

"Okay, our mom had to scrimp and work her fingers to the bone to afford? Not bloody likely. I have the title to that house. His deed doesn't mean jackshit."

"It meant something to the county clerk," I said.

"Fuck that noise."

"If you have the title, e-mail it to me, and I'll get it to the county clerk and explain things."

"Again. Fuck that noise. I'm here at Camp Pendleton. I'll be there tomorrow."

"You will?"

I was surprised.

"Goddamned right I will. I'll see you tomorrow, baby brother."

"What are you talking about? We're twins."

"Well I was born first. You're number two. So suck on that for a while, why don't you."

In an instant, I was looking at a dark screen.

Well, that went well.

27

"Huh."

"What?" Kai asked after he swallowed his eggs.

"My phone's showing I have a message from the Down Home Diner."

"That's weird. Aren't you going to listen to it?"

"I try not to let electronics interrupt meals." I set my phone back down on the kitchen peninsula where we were eating, me on the kitchen side, and Kai across from me.

Kai laughed. "I'd say looking at your phone and seeing that you have a message, proves that you're already failing at your goal."

I wanted to stick my tongue out at him, but God only knew where that would lead us. Time to deflect.

"What time do you think Beau will get here?"

"Don't know. Your guess is as good as mine."

I spooned up more of my yogurt. Kai's phone rang.

"Does your rule apply to me?"

I shrugged. "It never applied to Sue when we lived together, so it shouldn't apply to you."

He grinned and answered his phone.

When it wasn't Beau I stopped listening, instead I finished up my yogurt and took Kai's and my dishes into the kitchen and rinsed them off. I'd put them in the dishwasher, after I unloaded the clean dishes.

"Hey, that was Simon. He's worried."

"Why?"

"He put an alert out on Senator Thompson. Turns out that he flew into McGhee Tyson Airport."

"So?"

"Sweetheart, that's the airport you fly into if you want to get to Jasper Creek."

"Oh. I didn't know that. I drove." I leaned on the kitchen counter. "That doesn't make any sense. What would a West Virginia state senator be doing out this way?"

"Simon and I figure it has to have something to do with you."

My gut clenched. "Do you think he wants to kill me?" As soon as the words were out of my mouth, I knew I was wrong, so I held up my hand. "Wait. Wait. I know. I'm wrong. He doesn't want to kill me. He wants my phone and all copies of the video."

Kai nodded.

"But why come to me directly? Why not send another goon?"

"That's what has Simon and I stumped. Neither of us think he would want to get his hands dirty."

"Hmmm. When did he arrive?"

Kai came around the peninsula into the kitchen. "Just now."

"How long does it take him to get here from there?"

He pulled me into his arms. "An hour. But you don't have anything to worry about. He won't get to you."

I rested my cheek against his chest. "I know." I placed a kiss on his cotton-covered chest. "Trust me. I know."

"This will work," I told the three men standing in front of me.

"I don't like it. We don't know what he's capable of," Kai said for the umpteenth time.

"You're the one who told me, he told the guy in jail that he was pissed that the truck driver tried to kill me." I turned to Roan. "Isn't that what he said?"

Roan nodded. He was grinning. He thought I had a good plan. It was Simon and Kai I still had to convince.

"That doesn't mean he doesn't plan to hurt you," Kai pointed out.

"Have you seen a picture of the man?" I scoffed. He was teeny-tiny.

"Marlowe, that doesn't matter. If someone is mad, and they've planned ahead, they can hurt you," Simon pointed out.

"What can he possibly do to me while the three of you are in hiding in the house, waiting to pounce if he makes one wrong move?"

"Marlowe—" Kai started.

"Look, you two," Roan said. "If the three of us can't protect her, I'd say we're a piss-poor security agency. Especially since we have a fifteen-minute head start, surveillance equipment, and it's three to one-half."

I giggled. He was right about the one-half.

"I still say he could talk to me instead," Kai grumped.

"For the love of God," I burst out. "This is a good plan, and it will spike his wheels once and for all. Just get all your little spy shit, plant it around the living room, and let me confront the weasel. I want this over with."

Kai stepped up to me and put his arms around me. "Okay, we'll get our spy shit, and place it all around. You go get him, Tiger."

I grinned.

"We're going to need popcorn, you know that, don't you?" Roan said over my receiver.

"What in the hell are you talking about? Marlowe

could get hurt, and you're making it sound like we're going to see a show." The man was getting on my nerves.

"Marlowe's like my Lisa," he responded. Roan was on the east side of the house, at the window that was slightly open to the living room. He had a gun trained on the center of the room.

"And my Trenda," Simon chimed in over my receiver. Simon was in the back bedroom.

"What does that even mean?" I grumbled into my mic. I was in the kitchen pantry. I had a gun trained on the center of the living room as well.

"It means your woman has smarts and guts. She'll do fine," Simon explained.

"I don't want her to have to do fine. I want this mess to be over with, so she can just sit in her porch swing, drink iced tea, and get ready for the school year."

"Don't we all," Roan sighed. "Life doesn't always work out that way, that's why they've given us women who have balls and brains."

The doorbell rang. Marlowe took her time getting up off the couch and going to the door. She looked through the peephole and asked who it was.

"Can any of you hear what he's saying?" I asked the men.

"Negative," they both said in unison. That was a problem. I hoped for the sake of the plan, we could hear them once he was inside.

Marlowe opened the door and swung her arm

wide for the small man to come in. "What can I get you, Mr. Thompson? Would you like a glass of water? A soda? Lemonade? Some iced tea?"

"Iced tea would be lovely, Ms. Jones. Thank you."

"Simon, are you getting this?" I asked Simon.

"Yep. I'm just waiting for her signal."

"You have a lovely home. It's a shame you had to leave your home in West Virginia."

Marlowe walked by me to get to the fridge. I watched as she pulled out the pitcher and then poured the asshole a glass of tea.

"Would you like sugar?"

"Four teaspoons, please."

Marlowe didn't add any. Then she brought out the tea to the dining room table and motioned for the senator to sit down. Just like we'd all discussed.

"Thank you," Teddy said, as he took a sip and grimaced.

"What is your daughter planning on doing to make up the time she missed?" Marlowe asked as she twirled her hair.

"We already got her caught up with a private tutor. You don't have to worry your pretty little head about that. She told me you were a very conscientious teacher. I'm sure it must bother you to think that as you rightfully press your suit against Principal Sykes, you might also be spotlighting a child's innocent prank and opening her up to ridicule."

I heard Roan stifle a laugh. God, this tool was

unbelievable. I'd seen the video and his daughter was a little snake.

"Your daughter was filming a girl being beaten. The girl was being repeatedly kicked, over and over again. Your daughter did nothing to stop it. She stood there, filming the whole incident, giggling the entire time."

"You must be mistaken." He sat up straighter in his chair. "My daughter is a good girl. She would never bully another girl."

"She continued to laugh as this girl was pulled down the school hallway by her hair. What do you think about that?"

"I'd say you're lying," the man sputtered.

Marlowe pulled out her cell phone and slammed it down on the table. "Here, let's see the footage, and then you tell me who's lying. Your daughter, or me."

Sounds of a young woman giggling filled the room. You could also hear the faint sound of someone saying, 'Please stop.'

"Do you know who's giggling? Your daughter."

"You can't prove that," the senator said.

Marlowe picked up her phone and fiddled with it.

"Here's the good part. Let's listen to your daughter, Cindy. The girl who filmed this. Shall we?"

"No way. This is my phone and I'm not giving it to anyone. Just wait 'til I put this up on the internet. I'll get so many likes."

"Give this to me, now."

"You don't have the right to take it from me. I'll tell my parents. You'll lose your job."

"Give that back to me, that's my property."

"That's not your daughter's finest moment."

The senator slapped his hand down on the table, hard.

That must have hurt.

"I want your phone and all copies of that video." The senator was beyond pissed. "Now."

"You're not going to get it."

I could hear the satisfied smile in Marlowe's voice.

"One hundred thousand dollars for your phone and I watch you delete all your back-ups. Right now. I have the money in cash, in my rental outside."

"Do you know that the girl they were kicking, the girl who they dropped on her head, ended up needing to stay in the hospital for five days? I'm not taking your stinking money. It would make me happy to see your daughter and the other two girl brought up on assault charges."

He leaned over the table and shouted in her face. "One hundred and fifty thousand dollars."

"If you carry that much money around with you on your trips, I say we make it a cool quarter of a million dollars. Don't you think that's worth it to you, so that all your constituents don't find out that not only is your sweet little baby girl a terrible bully, but also so they find out that you hired someone to kill me?"

"You'll never be able to prove it," he stammered.

"I might not be able to prove that you hired someone to drive me over a cliff, but the guy you hired to kidnap me is in jail and he's talking."

"In your dreams, lady. I've paid him off. The lawyer I hired for him is the best. Even if he doesn't get him off, it'll be a light sentence. I'm paying this guy to keep his mouth shut, and he wants the cash."

I watched Marlowe lean back in her chair and cross her arms. She had a shit-eating grin on her face. "There's one last thing, senator."

"What? You want more than a quarter of a million? I didn't bring more than that. And I'm not going to pay you more than that."

Marlowe twirled her hair, signaling us again, and I stepped out of the pantry. "No, the last thing is, smile, you're on a livestream."

"What are you talking about?"

He looked around and saw me. Then he turned again and watched Simon walk into the living area from down the hall. Roan was climbing in from the side window.

"Did you get everything, boys?" Marlowe asked. She sounded exuberant.

"We got it taped, and it went live to his website,

and all his social media and to YouTube. He's already getting likes and comments. I bet this is going to be his most popular post." Simon smiled grimly.

"How exciting," Marlowe said as she threw her fist in the air.

28

My shoulders hurt. I didn't want to tell Kai; he'd be more upset than he already was. He was still kind of on a rant about me confronting Teddy the Turd, even though Nash already had Teddy in lock-up since the stupid bastard confessed to everything. Personally, I was thinking that he was upset because he didn't know where Arthur was and he was going to be meeting Beau. When I mentioned that, he'd kind of ranted that I was wrong, so I'd backed off and gone to the porch to text Sue. She told me that type of male behavior was normal, especially if they were really male-males. She knew from personal experience. Since I really adored Steve and the way he treated her otherwise, and Kai acted the same way, I figured I could put up with deflected ranting.

"Sweetheart?"

I looked up from my phone to see Kai on the porch looking at me with an apologetic expression.

"Yeah?" I responded as I shut down my text message with Sue.

"I'm done being a cranky asshole, in case you want to come back inside. I'm sorry."

I looked down at my phone.

"According to Sue, you're supposed to be a surly bastard for at least three hours. You didn't even last for two. I'd say this bodes well for our relationship." I grinned.

"Surly bastard, huh?"

I nodded as I untangled myself from the porch swing and preceded him into the house. He had the air conditioning on and I liked it.

"What do you say we go visit Chaos?" he suggested.

"You don't have to twist my arm for that. I already called Kizzie and she thinks she can come home a day sooner than expected."

Kai pulled me into his arms and kissed the end of my nose. "That's great news, Baby," he whispered.

I let out a shaky sigh. "I know. Not having her with me, hurts."

"She's your baby. Of course it hurts."

I bit my lip. It was probably too soon to ask something like this, but fuck it all, I needed to know. "What do you think about babies?"

"Babies of ours, or babies in general?"

I didn't answer. He was a bright man, he knew what I was asking.

"Okay, Marlowe. If this goes the way I'm almost a

hundred percent sure this is going, I'm all in for babies of our own. How old are you?"

"Almost twenty-eight?"

"The reason I'm asking, is that I don't want you having babies when it's not healthy for you. Especially not when there are plenty of babies around the world to adopt. Trust me, I've been all over this world, and I've met the orphans who need homes."

I was pretty sure my ovaries just exploded. I grabbed him around his neck before I had a second to think, then I let go. I cupped his cheeks. "God, how can I love you more every single second of every single day? I just want a big family with you. It's why I went into teaching. I love kids. I love seeing them learn, grow, and flourish. Being a mother, having a family again. Well. It means the world to me."

Kai blessed me with the sweetest kiss of my life.

"Giving you a family again means the world to me, Marlowe."

I wanted to stay close to the house so that Beau could find us. The fact that there was a bed close by might have been another reason that I liked staying close to the house. My cooking repertoire left something to be desired, but Marlowe had a wok and all the fixings for stir-fry, so this I could do. The bummer was that she didn't have any Asian noodles, but I improvised and went with spaghetti noodles instead.

I was trying to be quiet, because Marlowe had passed out. Her taking down Teddy the Turd then spending an hour with Chaos and then having drinks with Trenda, Lisa, Roan, Simon and me wore her out.

And maybe the sex.

I grinned. Yeah, possibly the sex. Okay, probably the sex.

Shit.

I sucked the web of my right hand, where the grease had spit up at me. Apparently, I needed to concentrate a little more on cooking, and a little less on sex.

Then I heard the slow sound of the slide guitar that was the intro to 'Free Bird' and I picked up my phone. Big Brother wasn't FaceTiming me, just calling.

"Is the shitty Canyon truck outside yours?"

"Whose truck are you calling ugly?" My heart was beating a mile a minute. Beau was outside. I turned off the gas on the two burners and headed for the front door.

"Marlowe has too much good sense than to buy herself an orange truck."

"It was a hell of a deal. I just needed to get from point A to B, and to haul shit. It does that."

I flung open the door, and there was Beau. In the flesh. Standing right in front of me.

He wasn't wearing a uniform. He was wearing civvies. Shit, we were both wearing light blue t-shirts and jeans, only difference was he was wearing a ballcap. He pulled his off.

"Brady," he breathed out the name.

I just nodded. I didn't correct him. Because who was standing in front of me was Grady.

His eyes widened.

"Fuckin' Brady!"

A smile burst across his sunburned face, his teeth bright white. The next thing I knew, he caught me up in his arms and lifted me off the ground. It hurt. But I didn't give a shit.

"Grady!"

I wiggled out of his hold and then we both had our hands on one another's shoulders. I felt tears threatening.

"Do you know how many times I'd be in our bedroom and wish for you to come home?" Beau asked in a whisper. "It was every damn day for years."

What could I say to that?

He grinned.

"And you're here! You're on our porch! Fuckin' A, Brady. I never thought—"

He stopped.

"I never thought..."

He used the bottom of his t-shirt to swipe at his eyes.

"I just never thought I'd see you again. Man, I thought you were dead!" He slapped me upside my head.

"Stop that!"

We both turned to see Marlowe wearing one of my tees that hit her mid-thigh, as she came storming through the living room to the front door.

"Don't you dare hit Kai. He has neck and back injuries, hitting him upside the head isn't good for that."

Beau looked askance. "Seriously, Bro?"

"It's nothing."

"It's not nothing," Marlowe said. "You told me." She came closer and slipped one arm around my waist and her other hand crept up over my heart.

"Fuck. You work fast, Brady. When did you get to town? A week ago?"

"I got here six weeks ago. Don't cast aspersions against Marlowe. She's my woman, and we're heading someplace serious."

Beau held up his hands, palms out. "Sorry, Marlowe, no offense meant."

"None taken." She smiled. "How about we take this soiree inside?"

It was then that I noted he had a pack on the porch beside him. "What's that?" I asked.

"It's all the paperwork that Bernie's ever sent my way. In it is the title to this property. Dad can go suck—" He looked at Marlowe. "He can go suck eggs."

"Well, let's bring it on inside and take a look. Marlowe, you can go get dressed," I suggested.

"It's just your brother," she protested.

"Yeah. Well, I think I have an idea how he thinks, so do me a favor and get dressed."

She rolled her eyes, but sauntered back to our bedroom. *Damn.* She looked just as good going as she did coming. I looked over at Beau and saw that he was thinking the same thing.

"I'm guessing you were wishing you came home sooner." I chuckled.

"Nah. I knew what I wanted, and those days are over. I had my chance." He sighed as he put his pack on the dining room table.

"You want dinner? I've made stir-fry."

"I could eat."

There were six beer bottles on the table, and I had never had more fun in my life. Scratch that; I had definitely had more fun in my alone time with Kai. But seeing these two brothers getting a chance to get to know one another was magical. There were so many parallels in their lives. As a matter of fact, there were two times when they were in the same country at the same time, and they would have met

one another except for small little chance circumstances.

Beau admitted that he had passed out at the exact
moment when Kai had been shot. He'd been in the
middle of physical training, otherwise known as PT.
Everybody thought it was sunstroke, but he'd never
experienced anything like it before.

"It took me a week to recover," Beau said.

"It took me almost a year to recover." Kai
laughed.

At eight-thirty there was a knock on the door.
When I got up to go get it, both men stood at the
same time. In the same voice, at the same time, they
told me to stay put. I would have been offended, but
I was too stunned to see them act as one person, so I
giggled instead.

They both stalked over to the door.

"Who is it?" Again, both of them spoke in unison.

"It's Lettie Magill. Kai, let me in."

Kai opened the door.

She took two steps into the house and stutter-
stopped. She looked from one man to the other. She
then turned to Beau and grabbed him. "It's so good
to see you back home."

Kai looked over his shoulder at me. I shrugged. I
didn't know how she did it either. I mean, I could tell
them apart, but how Lettie was able to do it, was
beyond me.

"Are you home to stay?" she asked as she finally let
go of Beau.

"Still have some time left to serve," he told her.

"Oh." She nodded her head. "You here because of your sumbitch father?"

"Yep."

"You're going to be able to stop him, right?"

"Damn right."

She peeked around Beau to look at me. "You didn't call my ma. She has news."

I got up from the table and walked over to her. "I'm sorry, things got out of hand."

"I can see that," she smiled. "Ma remembered that old Willie Ames was a good friend of your daddy back in the day. Do you remember him?" She looked between Beau and Kai.

Kai shook his head, and Beau pinched the bridge of his nose. "I think I remember him coming around and bothering Mama from time to time."

"Greasy gray hair, and he stank?"

"Yep." Beau nodded.

"He lives with an aunt of his, at the Blue Ash Village trailer park. Poor old Via, she doesn't deserve having someone like that sucking the life out of her. He's living off her disability money."

"Are you thinking that my dad—"

"Our dad—" Beau interrupted Kai.

"Our dad," Kai corrected himself. "Are you thinking our dad could be holed away with Greasy Willie at the trailer park?"

"It's worth a shot." Lettie shrugged. She pushed her hand into her pants pocket and pulled out a carefully folded piece of paper. "Here, this is Via's address and phone number. Please, if Arthur is there, make sure to keep any confrontation away from Via. She doesn't need any more strife in her life."

Beau reached out and patted Lettie's shoulder. "We promise."

She reached up and patted his cheek. "You always were such a good boy. Don't forget to stop by the diner. We all want to see you."

"I'll stop by, I promise."

29

"Got any bright ideas for a game plan?" I asked as I drove my supposedly shitty truck through town.

"Take the next left up ahead," Beau said.

"For someone who hasn't been here in fourteen years, you sure know your way around."

"Had a friend who lived here for a while. His name was Nolan O'Rourke. Best kid you could imagine. He had it really rough."

I nodded. Old friends weren't anything to sneeze at.

"Okay, we're coming up on it." Beau laughed. "I see the sign has finally given up the ghost. Not surprised nobody's fixed it."

A blue sign hung crookedly from one metal post. It read *Welcome To Blue* and that was all. The rest of the sign had broken off.

"Okay, Via's in Lot 41. If we go knocking on her

door, the bastard isn't going to come out easy," Beau said.

I pulled over to the side of the road, right before the entrance to the mobile home park. "That's why we call her. We tell her we're the gas company and there's a problem with her meter. She needs to come outside so we can show her what's wrong."

Beau looked over at me. "I'm supposed to be the oldest, and therefore the smartest."

"I've spent damn near a year plotting on my computer. Makes a mind agile."

"I guess so."

"Plus, I was Delta. We have it going on. You Raiders are nothing but brawn."

Beau flipped me the bird, and I smiled.

I took out my phone and held out my hand for the piece of paper that Lettie had given Beau. I made the call and prayed that she would answer.

"Hello?" It was a man's voice.

"Hello, this is Marcus Roberts from the gas company. I need to speak with Via Ames. Is she available?"

"I'm her nephew. Talk to me."

"She's the person on the bill. I need to speak with her."

"She's not available." Willie sounded belligerent as hell.

"I'm sorry, but I need to speak with her."

"I told you. She's not available." Willie was past the point of belligerent. Now he was pissed.

"Do you live at Lot 41?" I asked in a reasonable tone of voice.

"Yeah."

"Then maybe you can help me."

"That's what I told you. Talk to me."

"I'll be there in five minutes. I need you to check the reading with me at the meter. There have been some anomalies. We need to get this worked out, otherwise Ms. Ames' bill will be over a thousand dollars next month."

"Are you fucking kidding me? You guys are nothing but cheats!"

"We're trying to be pro-active. Meet me at the meter in five minutes."

"Damn right I will." He hung up the phone.

I looked over at Beau.

"I'm worried about his aunt," Beau said.

"Me, too."

"How do we get dad out of the house? If he's there?" Beau asked.

"We'll play it by ear."

Before we drove into the trailer park, I unlocked the tool chest in the bed of my truck, gave Beau the Colt, and I made sure my Glock was handy. I stopped the truck four trailers before Number 41 and let Beau out, then continued to Via's. A guy with long, greasy hair stood by the side of a single-wide trailer that had seen better days. He was shaking the gas meter. His clothes looked like they hadn't been washed in the past month. When he heard my truck, he turned around and scowled, then stomped over to me.

"Who in the hell are you?"

"I told you. Marcus Roberts. I'm with the gas company."

"Why aren't you wearing a uniform? Why aren't you in a gas company truck?"

"They laid off damn near everybody last year. Now they hired back a bunch of us scabs. Those higher-ups are nothing but assholes if you ask me."

"So, why are you working for them?" Willie asked.

"It's a job. Need to put food on the table for my kids."

Willie shrugged. "Guess so." He turned around and went back to the meter. "So how is the damn company trying to steal from me?"

"Let me show you. And it's a damn good thing I caught it. I'm telling you. They are trying to screw everybody."

"I hate all of them big companies." Willie spit out a big stream of tobacco juice that nearly hit my boot.

And he stank to high heaven.

"Look here." I pointed at the meter. I had no idea what I was pointing at. "Do you see how this is over here?"

Willie nodded.

"Well, this needle should really be way over here."

"Yeah, it should." He nodded. Great, we were bullshitting one another.

"So, because it's not, we're talking a thousand-and-nineteen-dollar bill."

"Are you fucking with me?"

"No sir, I am not."

"How are you going to fix it?" Willie demanded.

"I'm going to turn this in to my supervisor. There is no way that a trailer as small as yours could be using this much gas. Unless, of course…"

This might work.

"Of course, what?"

"How is everybody feeling inside?" I asked.

"We're doing okay. I guess."

"How about your aunt? She couldn't come to the phone."

Willie got a squirrelly look on his face. "You're right. She's been feeling a mite poorly. But I've been giving her cough medicine and making sure that she drinks water and stuff. That's what the old bat next door said to do. Bitch can't mind her own business. God, she doesn't see my aunt for five days, and she's up in my grill."

"Willie. Can I call you Willie?"

"Sure can, Marcus."

"Is there anybody else besides you and your aunt in the trailer?"

He looked at me, then his eyes shifted to the left. "Nope, just me and Aunt Via. Why?"

"Well, you're looking a bit peeked. And your aunt isn't feeling well. If there was someone else, I would just wonder about her or his state of health. It might be the reason for all the gas. You could have a gas leak under the trailer. It would spew just a little amount inside, so that it would make you sick." I paused as I saw his eyes get wide. "You don't smoke, do you?"

"Nah, just chew. And Via makes Arth—"

"Who?"

"Never mind."

"Well okay. I'm kind of worried. I think I should send out a real technician who can check under the trailer. In the meantime, I'm going to shut off the gas and suggest you get your aunt out of the trailer immediately. This is serious business."

I went over to the valve and shut it off.

Willie hot-footed back into the trailer. Almost as soon as he went in, dear old dad came rushing out. Beau was on him in an instant. Hell, I hadn't even seen him nearby.

"Kai, get the hell off me," Dad whined.

Beau picked Dad up by the back of his neck, cocked back with his right hand, and let loose. Dad was on the ground. Out cold.

"Well, fuck," Beau said disgustedly. He looked over at me. "Go in there and get some water. I'm not done with him."

I shrugged and looked over at the entrance. Willie was standing there, his head turning between Beau and me and back again.

"Get a pan of water," Beau yelled. He just stood there.

"Willie. Get a pan of water. Right fucking *now*," Beau yelled louder.

Willie darted back into the trailer. I went over to stand over Dad. I prodded him with the toe of my boot. Nope, he wasn't playing possum. Beau and I waited.

"Here."

Beau took the pan and poured it slowly over Dad's face. Dad started to moan.

"Get up, old man. I'm not done with you."

Dad got up on one elbow and squinted up. "Kai?"

"No, it's Grady. Now get your worthless ass up."

Dad slumped back onto the ground. Beau hauled him up onto his feet and punched him in the ribs. I remembered what Doc Evans had said about Arthur having broken Beau's ribs. I watched Beau whale on Arthur. Punch after punch, Dad groaned and begged him to stop.

"You want in on this?" Beau asked me.

I thought about it, and realized Beau had a lot more grievance. "He's all yours."

Dad's head lolled around like a broken doll, one eye shut. The only reason he was partially standing was Beau was holding him with one hand.

"You piece of shit. I don't know if what you've

done will get you in a jail cell, so let's do this, shall we?"

I watched as Beau kicked out at the side of Dad's knee. I heard the bone break and cringed.

"Jesus," I heard Willie whisper.

Beau dropped Dad onto the ground. He turned to look at Willie. "Did you see anything?"

"God no," he whispered.

"I want to check on his aunt. I think something fishy is going on," I said.

I pushed Willie out of the way and made my way into the trailer. I found the old woman in the back bedroom.

"Via?" I whispered.

She was in a house robe, shivering. She was barely conscious.

"Call an ambulance, Beau. I think there might be a prison sentence in these two assholes' future after all."

EPILOGUE

SEVEN MONTHS LATER

Lettie sure could put on one hell of a spread. It was a wonder that the picnic tables didn't come crashing down. And how many Magills were there, anyway?

I looked over at Marlowe, and this time she was holding a newborn. Simon and Trenda's little boy, Drake. She looked good holding a baby. She'd been holding kids every time I turned around. It was about time I did something about that.

"Hey, are you going to join the conversation, or just make cow eyes at your woman all afternoon?"

I glanced down at Sue Rankin. How great was it that I liked Marlowe's best friend?

"She's a pleasure to watch."

"You know I'm mad at you, don't you?" Sue asked for the umpteenth time.

"You might have mentioned it." I smiled.

Her husband put his arm around his petite wife's shoulders. "Quit busting the man's balls. Your friend can't help who she falls in love with. Anyway, they're buying a big enough house so that we can come and visit."

"Like those bedrooms are going to be empty for long," Sue groused.

I laughed. Sue had our number.

"The Whispering Pines is nice. And it has a room with a hot tub on the deck," Steve reminded her.

She relaxed against her husband. "There is that."

"Kai, get over here. Little Grandma wants to talk to you."

"Gotta go. When the queen asks for an audience, one must listen."

Sue giggled.

I sauntered over to the covered patio where Little Grandma was sitting with her two sisters and three of her daughters. I sat down at the table. "Hello ladies."

"Tell me, dear, do you think there is a chance that Beau will be here to stay?" Little Grandma asked.

I frowned. "There's no telling. It says something that for the last five weeks he hasn't let Bernie rent out his house."

Patty nodded. "That is a good sign. Why did you move out?"

"We wanted to give Chaos a bigger place to run around in and be closer to the forest."

Little Grandma reached over and put her hand on top of mine. "And you wanted the house to be free for your brother to come home to," she said gently.

"Now I want to know what happened to your daddy."

"You had to testify, didn't you?"

I looked at the woman who asked the question, and my mind went blank. Was this Gladiola or Ronnie?

"I'm Gladiola, honey. Gladiola Garner. I'm the second oldest. You'll see my kin all around town."

"Java Jolt. Ruby. Now I remember."

"Yep, she's my great-great-granddaughter. Now tell me about your daddy."

"He got put away for seven years for aggravated assault. Willie's trial is coming up."

"Didn't your daddy try to say that Beau hurt him?" Little Grandma asked.

"Yeah. He did. There wasn't any witness to testify to that, and I actually saw him fall down the three stairs from the front of the trailer. Doc Evans testified that all of his injuries could definitely be attributed to a fall, so they didn't believe Dad."

"Well, isn't that nice," Little Grandma beamed.

"Hey, Honey, can I get you a plate of food?" Marlowe asked me as she put her hand on my shoulder.

"I've already had one plate… But yeah, I could go through the tables again. Let's go together, shall we?"

Marlowe smiled down at me, and once again, I thought how lucky I was.

I couldn't wait until Beau showed up. Everybody was waiting for him. I wasn't sure how he was going to take to having the whole town officially welcoming him home, but he was just going to have to deal.

"Stuffed jalapeño poppers." Kai smiled as he put two on my plate.

I waved to Sam who was over at a table with Pearl and some of the other people who worked at her restaurant. She'd closed down for a couple of hours to come to the potluck. Now that I'd been here for almost a year, I was in the know about things. Like everybody else, I wondered when Sam was going to ask Pearl out on a date. The consensus was that after Sam's stroke, he should have had a little bit of sense knocked into him and would now pull his thumb out.

I waved to the Avery contingent. There was Trenda and Simon, with her sisters Evie, Zoe, Maddie and even Piper was here from San Diego. I needed to get over there before the evening was over and visit.

Kai moved us over to a table where Roberta was sitting with her husband and four boys. Forrest was the top student in my math class. He had shocked himself and his parents. When I had looked at his record in math it had been all D's and C's. My guess was nobody had ever challenged him in the past. The kid was a whiz.

"Hi, Ms. Jones. Do you want my seat?" Forrest asked as he stood up.

Kai gave me a hidden wink and I stifled a giggle.

"That's okay, Forrest, there's plenty of room," Roberta said. I noticed that Kai sat between me and Forrest, which made me want to giggle even more.

"Any word on how the lawsuit is going?" Roberta asked.

I shook my head. That was Jasper Creek. Everybody knew everything, and nobody was afraid to ask.

"I won," I smiled. "Principal Sykes was forced to offer me back my job."

Roberta looked stunned.

"It's okay, Ro. She's not taking it. She's taking a payout for wrongful termination instead. Ms. Jones is staying right here and continuing to teach at Jasper Creek High."

Roberta started to breathe again.

"Okay, now that I'm not going to have a heart attack, when are the two of you going to get married?"

"All in good time," Kai said. "All in good time."

"We found a house that we're going to buy, so no more renting. Score one for team Jones and Davies." I did a fist-pump.

"Where are you buying?"

"Out near Millie and Renzo's place. I'm going to get goats," I answered.

"Goats?" Forrest said.

"I don't know," I answered. "I just always wanted goats. They're so cute when they're little."

"And so ornery when they're big," Roberta's husband Tom put in.

I scrunched my nose. I looked down and saw I'd finished my plate. I turned to Kai. "Honey, I need to go let Chaos out." Unfortunately, our new landlord didn't let us set up a doggie door. But there *was* a huge space for Chaos to run around in.

"Okay. I'll go with you."

"We'll be back in an hour."

"Sure, they're going to go feed the dog," Roberta whispered to her husband.

I chose to ignore her.

Kai and I walked hand in hand through Lettie's back gate, promising everybody we'd be back. We also promised to let everybody know when we got word that Beau would be showing up.

Kai and I drove to our rental, which wasn't that far from the Whispering Pines. Roberta had been right, we were going back to the house for more than just a visit with Chaos. Kai had been on an out-of-town job for Onyx for a week, and had just gotten home last night. He'd been tired, but he'd put in a good effort, but we were both anxious for a little bit more alone time.

We hit the door, and if Chaos hadn't been right there to greet us, we would have been ripping one another's clothes off.

"Hi, baby." I crouched down. "Who's a good girl?"

Kai got down and gave Chaos a good rub too. Then he whistled, and Chaos followed him to the back sliding glass door. Kai threw out the chew toy and Chaos flew out the door. Nobody could ever know how relieved I was to see my dog healthy and happy.

"You good?" Kai turned around to look at me.

Okay, maybe Kai could. The man seemed to live in my head sometimes.

"I'll be better when I get you naked in the bedroom."

"I want to get *you* naked," he countered.

He held out his arms and I floated into them. Then we kissed. Kai's kisses were magical. Every single one of them was better than the one before. When I felt his fingers in my hair, massaging my scalp, another layer of pleasure engulfed me. Layer upon layer of mystical bliss.

He pulled me down until we were both kneeling on the floor, wrapped around one another. I was lost. This man was mine. My soulmate, who had somehow found me, cared for me, protected me, and loved me. As his lips tenderly played with mine I fought tears as I realized the bounty I had found.

He moved our arms until his hands held my hand.

"Look, Baby."

I looked into blue eyes that were hot like the center of the flame.

"Look down, Baby." He pulled at my hand.

I looked down and saw an ice-blue diamond on my finger.

"Marry me."

"God, yes. Forever yes."

Beau Beaumont

I pulled into the driveway of my house. There were a bazillion cars littering the streets. When I got out of my truck, I could hear the laughter coming from the house on the corner.

"Fuck."

I knew it was for me.

Why hadn't Kai warned me?

I watched the house in the twilight and saw the side gate open. Somebody was laughing as they took out a big plastic bag of trash.

"It's no problem, I've got it," she said.

"Thank you, Maddie."

I watched as Maddie Avery put the trash into the trash can. She'd grown up. She was my every dream come true.

I was fucked.

If you liked Dreaming of Home, don't forget to start at the beginning!

Finally Home by Kris Michaels
Time for Home by Maryann Jordan
Home Team Advantage by Abbie Zanders
Home Town by Cat Johnson
Dreaming of Home by Caitlyn O'Leary

Beau and Maddie's Story is coming out in Spring of 2025,
Grab a copy of Back To Our Beginning (Book 4) in Caitlyn's Jasper Creek Series.

If you like Caitlyn's Long Road Home Series, Pick up all of Her Jasper Creek Series, and meet some of her old Long Road Home Characters.

ABOUT THE AUTHOR

Caitlyn O'Leary is a USA Bestselling Author, #1 Amazon Bestselling Author and a Golden Quill Recipient from Book Viral in 2015. Hampered with a mild form of dyslexia she began memorizing books at an early age until her grandmother, the English teacher, took the time to teach her to read -- then she never stopped. She began re-writing alternate endings for her Trixie Belden books into happily-ever-afters with Trixie's platonic friend Jim. When she was home with pneumonia at twelve, she read the entire set of World Book Encyclopedias -- a little more challenging to end those happily.

Caitlyn loves writing about Alpha males with strong heroines who keep the men on their toes. There is plenty of action, suspense and humor in her books. She is never shy about tackling some of today's tough and relevant issues.

In addition to being an award-winning author of romantic suspense novels, she is a devoted aunt, an avid reader, a former corporate executive for a Fortune 100 company, and totally in love with her husband of soon-to-be twenty years.

She recently moved back home to the Pacific

Northwest from Southern California. She is so happy to see the seasons again; rain, rain and more rain. She has a large fan group on Facebook and through her e-mail list. Caitlyn is known for telling her "Caitlyn Factors", where she relates her little and big life's screw-ups. The list is long. She loves hearing and connecting with her fans on a daily basis.

Keep up with Caitlyn O'Leary:

Website: www.caitlynoleary.com
FB Reader Group: http://bit.ly/2NUZVjF
Email: caitlyn@caitlynoleary.com
Newsletter: http://bit.ly/1WIhRup

- facebook.com/Caitlyn-OLeary-Author-638771522866740
- x.com/CaitlynOLearyNA
- instagram.com/caitlynoleary_author
- amazon.com/author/caitlynoleary
- bookbub.com/authors/caitlyn-o-leary
- goodreads.com/CaitlynOLeary
- pinterest.com/caitlynoleary35

ALSO BY CAITLYN O'LEARY

Her Noble Protector (Book #7)

Her Righteous Protector (Book #8)

NIGHT STORM LEGACY SERIES

Lawson & Jill (Book 1)

BLACK DAWN SERIES

Her Steadfast Hero (Book #1)

Her Devoted Hero (Book #2)

Her Passionate Hero (Book #3)

Her Wicked Hero (Book #4)

Her Guarded Hero (Book #5)

Her Captivated Hero (Book #6)

Her Honorable Hero (Book #7)

Her Loving Hero (Book #8)

THE MIDNIGHT DELTA SERIES

Her Vigilant Seal (Book #1)

Her Loyal Seal (Book #2)

Her Adoring Seal (Book #3)

Sealed with a Kiss (Book #4)

Her Daring Seal (Book #5)

Her Fierce Seal (Book #6)

A Seals Vigilant Heart (Book #7)

Her Dominant Seal (Book #8)

Her Relentless Seal (Book #9)

Her Treasured Seal (Book #10)

Her Unbroken Seal (Book #11)

THE LONG ROAD HOME

Defending Home

Home Again

FATE HARBOR

Trusting Chance

Protecting Olivia

Isabella's Submission

Claiming Kara

Cherishing Brianna

SILVER SEALS

Seal At Sunrise

SHADOWS ALLIANCE SERIES

Declan